THE TRIAL OF
MAGGIE
METRONIA

A BONE ISLAND MAGGIE MYSTERY
BOOK 3

The New Atlantian Library

Manhanset House
Shelter Island Hts., New York 11965-0342

bricktower@aol.com • absolutelyamazingebooks.com

Library of Congress Cataloging-in-Publication Data
Gregory, Peg.
The Trial of Maggie Metronia. A Bone Island Maggie Mystery, Book 3.
p. cm.

1. FICTION / Mystery & Detective / Women Sleuths.
2. FICTION / Mystery & Detective / Amateur Sleuth.
3. FICTION / Humorous / General
Fiction, I. Title.
ISBN: 978-1-955036-97-9, Trade Paper

November 2025

THE TRIAL OF
MAGGIE
METRONIA

A BONE ISLAND MAGGIE MYSTERY
BOOK 3

Peg Gregory

**The New
Atlantian Library**

Habent Sua Fata Libelli

COMMENTS AND REVIEWS OF PEG'S BOOKS

Starfish

"Peg Gregory paints visual images of the settings that are so real I can almost smell the Sargasso weed washed up on the beaches . . . strong visual images both of her characters and of the locale, which in this novel comes to life as strongly as her people."

—*Writer's Digest*, Cincinnati, Ohio

"I just finished Starfish and I loved it . . . wonderful and touching love story brought tears to my eyes. Peg has a wonderful talent for evoking true emotion from the reader."

—Alison McKinney, teacher, Houston, Texas

And Then There Was One, A Memoir

"A fascinating account of nursing in mid-century America . . . the extraordinary story of a remarkable, dedicated lady."

—Joanna Brady, author *The Woman at the Light*

"Veritably a bible of nursing history from 1955 until recent times . . . rich narrative."

—C. S. Gilbert, Solares Hill, Key West Citizen,

and author *Mother Poems*

DEDICATION

For my great-grandchildren, Kadence, Lillie, Peter, Marco, Owen, Liam and Elsie, I love you dearly and I'm so very proud of all of you! Only one of you is too young now to read books, but she loves to look at them and it seems she's reading them, so who knows, maybe she is. She certainly loves to be read to, don't you, Elsie! I hope you all love books as much as I do, which is why you always get a book on your birthdays and Christmas, no matter what else I give you. When you read, you will visit many places and see many things in your mind's eye you might never see, otherwise. Books are meditation for the mind and nectar for the soul. I might not always be with you, but books will be, so always enjoy them.

—With my love always, Grandma Peggy

Other works by Peg Gregory

Starfish

And Then There Was One, A Memoir

The Bone Island Maggie Mystery Series

Bone Island Maggie, book one

Murder in Windsor Park, book two

The Trial of Maggie Metronia, book three

"You're a nosy sleuth like me because you can't help it."

—Alma, in 'Sweet Betsy' by Ed Lynskey

ONE

"What if it's all fiction? What if the men of that day made it all up to keep everyone in line, like – well, like women, for instance? I mean, look at all the rules they had for women, Carolyn. I'm sure they had good fiction writers in the early days as they do now. Why couldn't they have used them to make it all up to suit them and the rules they laid down to keep women acting just as they wanted them to, so the men could keep all the power?"

Her companion on the terrace just shrugged and smiled at her. When Maggie Metronia got on a roll, she ran with it and barely took a breath. The two women lived in the same house and often ended up in the evening watching the sunset together from Carolyn's porch, since it was higher and they could see the ocean and horizon from it.

"Just look at all those rules for women in the Bible, Carolyn. They couldn't let men other than their husbands see their hair, so they kept it covered with a scarf whenever they were away from home. They were subservient to men, they were men's property, and they darned well couldn't let other men see what their husbands saw, nor even an elbow! They couldn't cut their hair, wear jewelry or makeup, which in that day was probably just kohl on their eyelids. They sure couldn't wear anything considered skimpy, despite how hot it was in the Middle East, and as far as we know, that's where most of them lived during those days. As much of their bodies as possible had to be covered, just as the rule is in parts of the Middle East today for the female population. I can't begin to imagine having to wear a burka here on the island or any other place where the temperatures can get to the 90s or above. And those stories about little children being sacrificed – what if it was just fiction to make their children behave?"

"Oh my goodness, that's really a deviation for you, isn't it?"

"What do you mean, a deviation – from what?"

"Well, it sounds like you're saying now that you don't believe there's a higher power, God. I thought you had loads of faith."

"No, that's not what I'm saying at all. I still think God exists. I can't look at a baby, a newborn animal, a plant that springs from the ground, any living thing, and think there's no God. I don't think we just – that it's all some kind of accident. And that's not negating the 'big bang' theory. It could have looked like an accident, but maybe it wasn't. Who are we to say what happened to start all this?"

"Okay, that sounds more like Maggie Metronia." Carolyn Cramer smiled at her friend, as they watched the sun set over Key West on a Friday night from Carolyn's third story terrace in Maggie's large historic home on United and Duval streets.

Maggie laughed. "Oh, it does, does it? Well, that's how I feel about it. And I don't think this is all there is, either. When people say to me, what if when you die, there really is nothing more, I say fine, but I'd rather believe this isn't all there is and be happy I was right than not to believe at all. That would be depressing and I couldn't live that way. And if I'm wrong, if when my eyes close for the final time and that's that, no more me, I won't know there's nothing else, because I won't be aware of another thought. Right?"

"That's some pretty heavy stuff, Maggie dear." Her housemate always worried when she started talking about death and dying. She was only in her early 70s, but Carolyn supposed anything could happen to her heart or she could get cancer or some other fatal disease.

"Yes, I suppose it is, but to me it's important stuff. I think we're all spiritual beings and when we die, I think what makes us 'us' lives on. Where that is, I don't know. Maybe we just live on near our loved ones, but they can't see us because we're ethereal beings after we die. Or, maybe the whole universe is our home after we die. Maybe we're not confined to one place at all, but now that we have no physical body to weigh us down, we can just go anywhere we please as spirits, as well as stay near our family when they need us. Maybe the whole universe is Heaven. I don't pretend to know what will happen, but that's what I'd like to happen, that when we die we're free to go anywhere we like whenever we like, including right here near the people we love."

"So," a voice behind them said, "when I die, you think I can stay around the two of you, eh, Mag? That right now there could be fifty other people sitting out here on the terrace?" He chuckled, but Maggie didn't think it was funny at all.

"Laugh all you want, Homer Wiley, but you can't prove me wrong, any more than I can prove me right," she told him.

"Come on out, Homer, join the party," Carolyn said to the third member of their chosen Key West family, as she gave him a big smile.

"Yes, you might as well get in on the discussion, and put your two cents worth in since you already heard part of it." Maggie dearly loved their friend, even though he irritated her to no end at times. He'd been her best friend since she was a much younger woman, sitting on the dock at Mallory Square listening to him play his bagpipes. He was only in his twenties then, out of the Marines just a few years and still very much in the Marine mode, with the crew cut he still wore, albeit a silver one now. When she met him, she was nearing forty, but looked twenty. She had a trim hourglass figure and long naturally blonde hair, and a smile that turned every head around them. She had beautiful pearly white teeth and every time she smiled at him, Homer felt special because he was her friend and that's the way she felt about him. They were almost inseparable, always heading down to their favorite bar after sunset to sit there, eating peanuts or something heavier and drinking that Sam Adams beer, while they talked with each other or others around them.

As she got older, she began to have problems with her gums and started losing her upper teeth, and even though the dentist worked hard to restore the health of her gums, he could do nothing about the teeth that had come out or had already loosened until she had no upper teeth at all. Homer and Carolyn had given up trying to get her to go to Big

Pine Key where that nice Dr. Troxel, whom she really liked, wanted to put implants in so she could have upper teeth again, since she had all her lower ones. He told her she had good bone, so with implants she could have her smile back that everyone missed. But her, it seemed. Maggie was such an intelligent woman, but somehow she had gotten it into her head that there were microchips in dental implants by which the CIA could track people and she told the nice dentist that "no durned CIA was going to track" her.

Now that she was a wealthy woman, having won Power Ball several years ago, Homer was her chauffer. He loved Maggie like an older sister might be loved if he had an older sister, which he didn't. They both loved Carolyn Cramer, but Homer did not love *her* like a sister. She was having none of it, though, to his constant disappointment.

"So what's this about us flying around the universe after we die? Do we have space ships and astronaut suits or are we just white wispy ghosts flying out there dodging planes, drones and Kim's rockets from North Korea? Or do they just fly right through us?" He winked at Carolyn, waved his hands through the air to tease Maggie, knowing he'd probably get her dander up before it was over.

"You can tease all you want, but one of these days you might find out I wasn't totally wrong. I don't know how it's going to work, but I do know these minds were not created for nothing. I think they're going to go on and on and on, and never die."

"Oh, so it's not our souls or our spirits that will live on, but our minds?" He scratched his silver crew cut as though seriously puzzled.

"Oh stop." This made Carolyn and him laugh. "I don't know if it will be our minds and our souls that make up our spirits, but I just don't think dying is the end of us, young man."

"But what about people like Hitler and Mussolini? They sure did a lot of horrible things, Mag. Do you think they get to fly around Heaven all day like the rest of us who've tried not to hurt others in this life?"

"Oh, I don't know. Seems like they shouldn't, doesn't it. They couldn't hurt anyone again without their physical bodies, but seems like there should be some consequence for what they did in their physical lives, doesn't it." Her face brightened then, and she added, "Hey, maybe their punishment is that they didn't get to live on, that when they died, that was the end of them, period."

"So, they weren't sent to a place where they're being punished eternally?"

"How should I know, Homer? That might be fiction, too. I just don't think they should get to enjoy what the rest of us get to enjoy, do you?"

He laughed and said, "Well, no, and I think ceasing to exist would be a great way to repay them for all the atrocities they committed against other humans while they were on earth. If there isn't a fiery underworld somewhere that they get sent to, that is. Naw, I think denying them the right to continue as spirits would be great punishment for them and people like them. Not that they'd know it. But I'm not God, am I."

"Do you want to know what else Maggie has concluded about everything?" Carolyn grinned at Homer and his stomach had those butterflies women talk about when the love of their life looks at them. He coughed to cover what he was experiencing. She was beautiful when she smiled that way. She was beautiful, period, no matter what she was doing. Even in her fifties.

"Sure, might as well tell me all of it," he said when he stopped faking the cough.

When she told him about Maggie's believing most of what they'd read all their lives might be fiction to keep women and children in their place – subservient and unseen – he laughed. "Well, our Maggie, you've really been doing a lot of thinking about all this, haven't you?" Homer had Scottish ancestry and every now and then his talk was old Scottish. He didn't seem to notice when he did it, but they did. They just smiled and said nothing.

"Yes, I have, and I think I'm right about it. And I think Jesus loved women and children and that he put a stop to all the nonsense when he grew up. I think he was our kind of people, real and kind to everyone except those who hurt others, and then I think he had a temper toward them." She stopped for a moment to take one more look at the sunset that was painting their sky a reddish purple. They turned to look at it, too, and none of them said a word because this was what they lived to see every evening and when they were given such a beautiful scene, they each centered on it no matter what else was going on.

After it began to fade a bit, Maggie said, "And on that beautiful note, I have a roast to check in the oven, so I hope you two are going to join me downstairs later." She got out of her wicker rocker, moved her back in a circular way she had of relieving the stiffness and without another word, headed back through Carolyn's apartment to go down to her own on the second floor. They looked at each other with big smiles and Homer held out his hand for Carolyn to lead the way downstairs.

Maggie had already basted the pork roast in the oven, seasoned just as they all liked it. The aroma was strong but nice. When they walked into the kitchen, she turned and with that big toothless smile, she told them it would be about another twenty minutes. When she smiled, it occurred to Homer that had she only been right about microchips in dental implants and had she only allowed Dr. Troxel to put in those 'microchipped' implants after her kidnapping last year, they could have traced and brought her home right away. As it was, she brought herself home by foiling one of her kidnappers, while the other one who'd been so nice to her, drove her away to the highway where she was able to call the sheriff's office to tell them where to find her other kidnapper, whom she incapacitated with some nutty brownies laced with lots of a tasty chocolate product she'd found in their Granny's medicine chest. That was the comical story of the sheriff's office for quite a while, the 'X-Laxed kidnapper' foiled by none other than the Maggie they all knew and loved. She had been a guest of their jail when she and Homer were believed to have killed a friend and hung his body over the mangroves in Biscayne Bay across from Alabama Jack's on Card Sound Road. This was after they nearly got eaten by an alligator, stepping on him to get into the mangroves in the first place, thinking he was a floating log. To say they'd had their share of adventures was putting it mildly.

Carolyn busied herself with chopping the vegetables she wanted to put into a salad, while Homer was going through the baking potatoes to pick out the nicest ones to bake in the microwave to have with the pork roast. Maggie had added carrots and celery to the roast when she came downstairs from watching the sunset. This was how most of their evenings ended, with the three of them in the kitchen or two of them in the kitchen and Homer outside on the porch tending the yellowtail or some other kind of fish or meat on the grill.

All of a sudden, Homer said, as he got the scrubbed baking potatoes for the microwave from a large plate, "Oh, for heaven's sake, I forgot to tell you the big news!"

"What big news?" Maggie said, with Carolyn echoing her as she chopped the salad vegetables.

"We have a serial killer in the Lower Keys," he said, in the same way he'd say, I'm going to Publix in a little while. No excitement in his voice. Not even a worry in it.

"What?" Maggie said.

"What?" Carolyn echoed, holding the knife in mid-air. "Where did you hear that and when? How could you not tell us something like that?"

He shrugged, as though it were nothing. "It's big news, but with all the trouble you two have gotten into for the past three or four years, having another serial killer around doesn't seem that important. It sort of pales in comparison with the ones you knew."

"Oh Homer, just stop." Maggie said as she took the roast out and put it in the center of the breakfast table where they all preferred to eat dinner or a light supper.

"Don't 'oh Homer' me, when you know it's true. Do I have to elaborate for you what happens every time there's a murder on this island? You can't keep from getting involved, and you darn well know it." He laughed, and took the potatoes out of the microwave and set the plate on the table with the meat. On a more sober note he added, "And no, I haven't forgotten about Hamilton Jacques. I was the guy who put an end to him, remember."

Neither said a word as they remembered the horrible night that murderer tried to kill Maggie by slitting her throat right out there in the back yard before Homer signaled for her to pretend to faint and fall backward into the guy before she went down, so the knife wouldn't cut her and he could have a shot at him, followed by one from the sharpshooter from the police department that put an end to Jacques' life.

"And if I recall, Maggie isn't always alone in her sleuthing. Seems to me she had a friend who had a hand in it a time or two," he said, as he smiled at Carolyn.

As she set the big crystal salad bowl in the center of the table with the rest of the food, she said, "Hey, don't look at me. It's Ms. Instigator here who gets into things. I just go along to try to dissuade her from whatever it is she has her mind set on doing." That got a smile out of both of the others.

Maggie didn't usually say grace at the table, but when everyone had seated themselves in their usual spots around the small round table, she bowed her head. They looked at each other, their eyebrows up and then shrugged and bowed with her. "Dear God, thank you for that beautiful sunset you gave us tonight, for this wonderful meal we're blessed to have and please don't let that serial killer kill any more of the good people in the Keys before he's caught. That's all. Thank you."

The other two looked at each other again, and each one hoped Maggie would steer clear of this one. They really worried, as she somehow inserted herself right in the path of the killer every time there was a murder or several murders in South Florida or the Florida Keys. It wasn't always by choice, but she never seemed to shy from it, either. If ever there was a wannabe sleuth, it was Maggie Metronia, Bone Island Maggie to many on the island. Despite being in her mid-70s now, she was showing no signs of slowing down. She still rode her bright red adult trike all over Key West every day and it seemed trouble followed her wherever she went on that small 2 by 4 mile piece of rock.

"Hey Carolyn," she said, after she finished chewing a small piece of meat. "Is your mother okay?"

Carolyn put down her fork and looked at her. "Why, yes, she's fine. Why do you ask?"

"No reason, just haven't heard you mention her lately. You have talked with her recently, right?" She knew there was animosity between the two women, which was the main reason Carolyn lived on the island instead of in her hometown in North Carolina.

"Yes, mom," she answered with a chuckle. "I called her on Sunday, as a matter of fact. She's doing fine, just as irritating as always, if you must know."

"Is she still insisting you'd be safer living back home instead of here?" She gave up on the meat and was eating small pieces of the carrots and potato.

"Of course. Ever since Jacques tried to kill you in the backyard, she's harped on it, just knowing he has an evil twin who's going to grab me in a dark alley or something." She giggled and Maggie laughed with her.

Homer, who'd been too intent upon eating the fine roast pork and vegetables to talk much, stopped eating for a moment and took a drink of his Sam Adams, which he had with everything unless he was drinking coffee. "And how's the ex-husband and his young stripper wife – Bubbles, right?" he asked.

Carolyn laughed and said, "Delilah, Homer. And I have no idea how they are. Mother knows I'll hang up without another word if she even mentions them."

"You still carrying around that hatred over them?" Maggie never carried a grudge and could never understand why anyone else bothered.

"Oh, I don't hate them. I just don't care to hear about them. They deserve each other after the way they got together, right under my nose. I just have no reason to think about them or ask how they're doing. I'm sure Mother will break our agreement and mention his name if something happens to him – or if, heaven forbid, he becomes a father."

Homer chuckled and Maggie laughed, too. "Well, I guess that answers your question, doesn't it," she told him, as they all went back to their supper and forgot about Carolyn's ex-husband and the wife he picked up during Fantasy Fest one year when she was wearing nothing but body paint, everywhere.

"I have some news, too," Carolyn said. "We have a new doctor in town. Pass the rolls, please, Homer." After Homer passed the basket, she lifted the dish towel and chose a sourdough roll before covering the others. "Mag?"

"Oh, no thanks. One's enough for me. What kind of doctor? Seems like we have every specialty down here."

"You know, I can't really say. I forget who told me when I was standing in the line at the grocery store, but when I asked that same question, she just shrugged and said that no one seems to know."

"That's pretty strange, isn't it. Where's his office or does he have one, yet?"

"I don't know where it is or if he even has one."

Homer, who hadn't seemed to be following the conversation, said, "Over in that building that was vacant so long near the old Ben Franklin."

"Well, I'll be," Maggie said. "You knew all along there was a new doctor in town and didn't tell us, either. Or me, since Carolyn knew, too. Do you know what his specialty is, if he has one?"

"Nope, only heard he was a doctor and was having the building painted. I don't know if he's moved into it or not. Nor do I care. If there's anything we don't need more of here, it's doctors."

"Well, maybe he has an important specialty we don't have," she told him. "Like toenail doctor or something like that."

Carolyn grinned at her. "I think that's pretty well covered by podiatry, isn't it."

"I just threw that out there. And of course, I know the podiatrist treats nails, too. I'm just curious, though."

Homer and Carolyn looked at each other. They knew if anyone could find out what kind of medicine he practices, it was Maggie. They knew she'd probably make a point of riding her trike by there to get a look at the building, to see if there was a sign out, yet.

"Well, you let us know what you find out," Homer said, as he took another swig of his Sam Adams. Carolyn snickered and Maggie just got up to cut the Key lime pie she'd taken out of the fridge before they sat down to eat. She said nothing, but they saw her take a deep breath as she cut the slices and put them onto the dessert dishes. Homer knew she'd find out tomorrow and couldn't help but laugh. Maggie was anything but someone who minded her own business. She hated not knowing something. And she would find out, even if no one else knew. Carolyn swatted his hand so he wouldn't get Maggie upset.

"Okay, here you go, two Key lime pies coming up." She walked back to the table and set one in front of each of them, paying no attention to their talking and snickering about her.

"Wow, you really outdid yourself with this one. That meringue must be six inches high. And does it ever taste good." Carolyn was lavish always with her praise of her friend. Homer just smiled and continued eating his that was so delicious he barely took a breath between bites. No one in Key West, even the oldest real Conch could make a Key lime pie like his Maggie and he felt like the luckiest guy on the island as he ate more of it. When he met Maggie that first day on the pier, when she walked away from him, one of his cop friends started complaining about her, saying she claims to be a Conch when she didn't come to the island until she was 16. Homer just laughed and asked him what it hurt for her to say she was a Conch. He said, "It isn't as though someone got a prize if he's born on the island, is it?" The cop just moved on. Homer knew Conchs were special on the island, and he respected them, but when they acted like this one did, he couldn't help but tease them about it. Maggie told Homer years later that she heard him defending her and that's when she knew she had a real friend on the island. He smiled to himself remembering that day. He wasn't born on the island, either, but couldn't see any reason not to let her think of herself as a Conch if that's what she wanted.

TWO

"Hey Chief, have you met that new doctor, yet?" Lieutenant Blake Butler slammed the file cabinet closed after putting the last file into it.

"What new doctor?" Chief Lenny Doan was working on the budget and wasn't so much interested in a new resident of Key West as he was in making idle conversation to get his mind off the shortfall he was finding for the coming season. Seems he always had a shortfall and had to go begging for funds from the city commission.

"His name's Tobin and he's really a strange duck. Georgie and I went to dinner at the Sloane's last night and he was there. Young, good looking guy, but he sure didn't sound like any doctor I've ever met."

"How's that?"

"Well, whenever anyone tried to bring up anything medical to find out what his specialty was, if he has one, he'd always try to change the subject. Myra Sloane specifically mentioned all the pain Jack was having with that leg that was injured when he was broadsided on his bike last year."

"What did the doc have to say about it?"

"He said and I'll quote as best I can, 'I find that most pain is rooted in stress, that there's usually no need for pain pills or heating pads or anything else.' And then Georgie popped up with, 'So, how do you treat it then?'

Doan chuckled and said, "Leave it to Georgie to back him into a corner. What'd he have to say to that?"

Butler laughed and said, "He basically ignored her question. Just kept going on about how stress can really mess a person up these days. He talked in circles and never once answered a specific question anyone asked him."

"Well, that's not going to bide well on *this* island with specialists so in demand."

"No, I don't think it will. Are you about ready to wrap it up there? I'm getting hungry. I'll treat you to a rib eye at the Pier House."

"You're on, thanks. I'm getting nowhere on this and think I'm going to have to take it to the city commission Tuesday night."

"Oh boy, they aren't going to be too happy. They just said at the last meeting how everyone's going to have to tighten their belts, because with so many places having to close because of the pandemic, too many are asking for help and the money isn't going to last the year if it keeps up."

"Damn fools. It wasn't the fault of the people. No one wanted to shut their doors."

"I know that and you know that and most of the people on the island know that, but you also know how tight-fisted that commission is when it comes to spending any of the money set aside for emergencies."

"How well I know. Okay, I'm ready. Let's get out of here."

He was just following Butler out the front door when one of his sergeants rushed through it. "We have another strange death, Lu. Chief. Young woman like the others. Found her down across from the Bight office parking lot. Looked like she'd washed up from the lagoon."

"Cause of death unknown again?" Doan asked.

"Yeah, M.E. said there's no visible signs of trauma aside from small bumps and bruises from washing ashore."

"Did she have any idea how long she'd been in the water?"

"No sir, she said she won't know that till she gets her on the table."

"Well, doesn't sound like a homicide, so no need for us to go to the scene. Keep us posted if you hear anything on the street that convinces you otherwise. And tell the squad to keep particularly vigilant to anything that seems off. Was she local, by the way?"

"No, Lu, her wallet and purse were nearby and her license said she was from Long Beach."

"California? We don't get many Californians down here. Try to find out where she was staying, Spivey. Maybe she was relocating rather than just doing the tourist thing."

"Will do, Chief. You all headin' out for a bite?"

"Going to try to, wanna come?" Butler liked his sergeant, who worked way too hard most days.

"Thanks, but I'm going to grab a sandwich at my desk and make some calls. Enjoy!" He headed on through the doors and went upstairs to his desk, as the two of them got into the lieutenant's car to hopefully eat their meal in peace without interruption.

It almost worked, but a few minutes before they were ready to eat the dessert put before them, three layer chocolate fudge cake, Butler's cell buzzed. He sighed and took it off his belt. "Yeah, what is it, Spivey?"

"Smerda just called and said it wasn't an accidental drowning. She's calling it a homicide, but isn't quite sure how it was done, yet. She's still working on her and hopes maybe the tox screen will tell her what happened."

"Oh?"

I said to her, "If it's an overdose of something, it still could be an accidental drowning, couldn't it?"

"What'd she say?" Butler asked, as the chief ate his cake, with one ear to this side of the conversation, since Butler couldn't put it on speaker in a public place like the restaurant.

"She just said, 'Nope, it's a homicide, all right. I just have to prove it.'"

"Thanks for the update and let us know what she finds out." He disconnected and the chief stopped eating for a moment.

"Well, what's the verdict?"

Butler swallowed the cake in his mouth. "Homicide, but she can't prove it. She's waiting on the tox screen."

"Even if it shows an overdose, it still could be an accidental death," the chief told him.

"That's what Spivey said to Jones."

"And?" Like Homer, the chief didn't like it when Butler was cryptic, creating drama before his answer.

"Smerda said, quote, 'Nope, it's a homicide, all right. I just have to prove it.'"

"Well, when Smerda says it's a homicide, I believe it's a homicide. Let's head over there when we finish this cake. It sure is good, isn't it!"

Butler couldn't agree or disagree. His mouth was too full of cake.

Fifteen minutes later they were in the morgue, suited up, as the medical examiner was still working on the poor young woman who was found alone, dead on the ground by the water.

"Anything new? The chief asked her, as they walked to the table.

"It's the biggest puzzle," Dr. Amy Smerda told them. "Just like the other young women who were found by the water's edge. There's the usual bumps and bruising you'd expect to find if one was battered by the rocks in the water, but not one darned thing that tells me how they died. And no sexual assault, either, just like the others. And no, it wasn't by drowning, either. There's no water at all in her lungs, just like the others. No, chief, she was dead before she hit that water, just like all the rest of them. And if the tox screen does come back positive of something, it sure wasn't by her hand that it got into her blood stream. I hate to say it, but I think your serial killer has a brilliant mind. He's found a way to kill young women like her and leave no visible evidence of how he's done it. Remember the other young ladies had a large amount of Propofol in them and none of them turned out to be the kind of women who took drugs. None of them were even known to smoke pot. And there wasn't one puncture from a needle in the arms of any of them, the same as with her. Not a trace of one. So what were they doing with Propofol in their system? Beats the heck out of me, damn it!" She threw her gloves on the mayo table and walked into the shower room, leaving them standing while the attendant, Hank Jones, cleaned up around the table, after pulling the sheet over the young woman's head and rolling her back into the cabinet space.

"She's sure frustrated over this guy – or woman, it could just as easily be a woman doing these killings since there's no evidence of sexual assault."

"Yeah, Chief, this one's getting to her. I've never seen her like this before, and I've worked with her for the past thirteen years."

They were still for a moment and Butler said, "Maybe it's because of Darlene, her only daughter. Remember, she just graduated from Stetson, so she must be in her early twenties."

"Just like these young victims. Dang, that has to be the reason it's getting to her. Probably every time they bring another one in like this, she thinks of her daughter. Damn that monster! Whoever did this isn't going to get away with it. He's only killing women in the Keys, nowhere else that anyone has reported. So, we're going to find him. He's going to make a mistake with one of them and leave something of himself and we'll get him." The chief was getting angry. He did not like unsolved crimes on his island. It's supposed to be paradise, not a dumping ground for a cold-blooded killer.

"You got that right. We'll get him. I just hope it's before he has a chance to kill another young woman."

"The thing that bothers me the most about this is that none of them seem to have seen it coming, whatever he did. None of them has a bit of trace under their nails when they're brought in, like they put up a struggle. Not one thing that leads us to believe they knew they were going to die by his hands." He looked at the morgue assistant. "Tommy, did Doc say whether there was any petechiae visible?"

"Nope, there wasn't. Her eyes were nice and white, no sign of strangulation at all. And she looked with the magnifier all around her neck and there was not a sign of a ligature having been around it."

"I hate mysteries," Butler said, as he kicked at the leg of the Mayo table.

The chief chuckled then. "Son, I think you might be in the wrong profession, if you hate a mystery, since it's your job to solve 'em."

His lieutenant grinned, "Yeah, guess you're right. Well, we're gonna solve this one just like we do all the rest. He might be brilliant, but we're not exactly stupid. He's going down." He thought for a moment and added, "Or she's going down."

His superior clapped him on the shoulder. "That's more like it. Come on. We've got work to do."

THREE

Maggie did ride her trike into the little strip mall where the old Ben Franklin was located. She just had to know. Had to see for herself. She saw the shiny new paint job on the building near it that Homer was talking about and saw a sign painted on the window. All it said was Tobin, M.D., no first name, no specialty, nothing except Tobin, M.D. and she thought that was strange.

She got off her trike and moved it into the bike rack that had only two more bikes in it. She took the chain and combination lock out of her front basket and put the chain around the trike as she always did, weaving it in and out carefully, so the combination lock would be hard to get to for someone wanting to steal it.

She opened the door and walked in. "Hello," she said to the young woman behind the counter. She was on her cell phone and didn't even nod her head in acknowledgment of Maggie's greeting. Dang, you just can't get good help these days! In her day, it was customary for receptionists to receive visitors who entered their area. On the phone or not, good receptionists greeted the people who came to be served. That was their job. Too many times today some receptionists forget why they're there and totally ignore visitors, as this one was doing.

She saw another women sitting further across the waiting room, facing the window. She was deep into a story in a magazine and didn't look up, either, so Maggie said nothing to her, but took a seat facing the inner office, which wasn't really an office. It looked like a gymnasium, nothing around it but walls. No small offices, no equipment, just bare walls and bare floors. What the heck?

Then she noticed, that if she scooted her chair just a smidgeon to the left, she could see around the Japanese screens that separated the waiting area from that cavernous area. By doing that she could also see a young handsome dark haired man with just a shadow of a mustache above his upper lip. He was sitting in a chair facing another man. She assumed he was Dr. Tobin.

What is he doing? Is he counseling the other man, who seemed to be quite a bit older than he was? They were sitting so close that their knees nearly touched. Maybe he's a boyfriend or the doctor's father. No, doubt it would be his father. Why not meet him in the privacy of his home if it was his father. Maybe the doctor is a psychiatrist or psychologist, but then, if that were the case, why not have a private office? No psych patient would want to speak with his therapist in such a wide open space as that. No, that doesn't fit at all.

Maggie was so caught up in trying to figure him out that she didn't hear the young woman call to her. "I asked if I could help you with something, ma'am."

"Oh, excuse me, I didn't realize you were finished with your call," she told her.

"Well?"

"I beg your pardon?"

"I asked you a question."

"Oh, right," she said, getting out of her seat. She gave her a big toothless smile and asked, "Yes, could you tell me where – I'm looking for a dentist who does implant surgery."

"Does this look like a dentist's office to you? I think you need to leave and let me get back to work."

"Why no, it certainly doesn't," Maggie told her. "It looks like a gymnasium that's waiting for the basketball hoops to arrive. But, I'll leave and let you get back to – what kind of work did you say you did?"

"Why, I never! How dare you? This is a doctor's office and I've asked you to leave, so get out now." She stood with her hands on her hips.

"Whoa, Winnie! What's the problem? We don't speak that way to clients. I heard you all the way in my office!" The doctor smiled at Maggie who gave him her big smile back.

"She, she insulted us, Dr. Tobin. She said this looks like a gymnasium."

"Let's back up a bit, shall we," he said, with a smile planted on his face. "May I ask how we can be of help to you, Miss?"

"Thank you. Well, as I was trying to tell this young lady at the information desk, I . . ."

"This is not an information desk!" She said it in such a loud voice that the doctor told her with his hands to tone it down. Her face was glowing pink and she was huffing in anger.

"Oh, my mistake," Maggie said, and then she turned back to the doctor. "As I was trying to tell you when you so kindly asked, I'm looking for a dentist who does implant surgery and I thought this young lady was someone who gave out general information about these things."

He grinned at her, ignoring the fuming of his employee. "No, this is Winnie, my receptionist. I'm Dr. Tobin," he said, holding out his hand for Maggie to shake. She ignored the gesture, pretending to look back at his receptionist. She certainly was not going to tell him her name or shake his sinister hand.

"Well, I sure got that wrong, didn't I. I hope you'll accept my apology, Ms. Winnie."

"My name is just Winnie, and I suppose I'll accept it."

"There now," the doctor said, "that's a lot more civilized, ladies. And to answer your question, ma'am, I'm new in town and I'm sorry to say I don't have any idea where any of the dentists on the island have their offices. Winnie also is new. We just flew into town from Chicago a couple weeks ago. Winnie won't be staying. She's just here to help me set things up and then she's going back to her husband and twin boys," he said with a folksy smile.

"Oh, isn't that kind of Winnie to help you set things up. And twin boys waiting back home. How wonderful for you, Winnie. I'm sure they must be missing their mama. What things exactly are you setting up, if I might ask, Doctor?"

Still smiling, he was opening and closing his fists at his side. Maggie suppressed a giggle. "Doctor?"

"Oh, my mind wandered for a moment. I'm so sorry. I'm keeping my patient waiting." He held the door open. "I hope you have better luck the next time finding that dentist. I'm sure he'll be happy to help you get your smile back."

"Oh, I'm sure you're right about that – if I ever find him or her, that is. Well, I see that you're both very busy so I'll get out of here and let you get back to – it."

With that, she waved and left the office, taking her time getting over to her trike. What an interesting conversation that was. He never once offered to say what he was doing here, if anything. Just wait till Homer and Carolyn hear about this. She had her trike unlocked, and tossing the chain and lock into the basket, she climbed onto the seat and started for home.

She took the longer way home, along the Atlantic. It was beautiful today, with blues of the water meeting a perfect azure sky and she was exhilarated, as though seeing it for the first time. But that was nothing new for Maggie. Every time she rode by the ocean, she was seeing it with new eyes. It never looked the same to her. Out beyond the nearest waves she saw multiple white caps as though a storm were brewing that wasn't showing its face, yet. That was okay with her. Stormy or calm, that big endless ocean was always a wonderful mystery to her and she never tired of being near it, of looking at its many faces in wonder. She loved to watch storms in the far distance, even as it was calm and quiet closest to her. She could tell if it was stormy close to Cuba or the Bahamas just by how the sea looked in the distance.

Maggie had always been in love with the sea. Her family took the same cruise often when she was much younger and they all got to know all the officers and many of the crew on the small ship. One day when she was standing at the rail looking out to sea within a few feet from the young chief officer, a handsome lad from New Zealand, he said, "You love it, don't you."

"Are those stars up there in that black sky?"

He laughed. "I guess that means yes. Let me ask you something. You're still young and look able-bodied. Did you ever think of getting some sailor training under your belt and actually going to sea as a working member of the crew?"

She looked at him with wide eyes and a startled expression. "You mean I could be a sailor? Seriously?"

"Sure, why not? You would start as a sailor and knowing you as I've come to do, I wouldn't be surprised if you worked yourself up to an officer one day."

"Oh, chief, that has to be the nicest thing anyone ever said to me. What a dream that is for me, yes. I've always wanted to go to sea. I wouldn't want to be a doctor or nurse or one of those people charged with keeping the passengers entertained. I've always dreamed of being a real sailor on a big ship like this."

"Did you ever want to go into the Navy, Ms. Maggie?"

"No, that would be way too much discipline for me." His eyebrows lifted in surprise at that remark from someone not even out of high school.

He said, "Well, maybe so, but every ship has to maintain a certain degree of discipline. If it didn't, things would get lax and if there were an emergency, it wouldn't be handled too well."

"Oh, I know that and I understand it. I've watched these sailors at work enough to know you can't have one or two of them being sloppy. They have to work in unison or the job wouldn't get done right. And I suppose they have to be ready for any kind of emergency. But they seem to have time to have fun, too. I've looked down from an upper deck and watched them at their poop deck parties. They're not shy about having a good time. Which I'm sure they do on a Navy ship, too, during down time at sea, but I just think working a cruise ship or cargo ship would appeal to me, more."

"Don't mean to burst your bubble there, but no, you would not want to work a cargo ship. It is way too rough – workwise and sailor-wise for the likes of you. No, I think you'd fit right in on a cruise ship. I'd be as proud as anything to have you serve under me, Ms. Maggie. Why don't you give it some thought and if you decide that's what you really want to do with your life after you finish school, come back to see me and I'll give you all the information you'd need to start your training and after you've earned your certification to be at sea, if you'd like to work under me on this ship, hey, just come see me personally and I'll steer you to the agent to sign up. Okay? Deal?" He held out his hand and they shook on it.

"Thank you, Chief Marin, that's very nice of you and I appreciate it. I will give it some thought, too. Well, I'll let you get back to work. I'm sure I'll see you again before the end of the voyage. Have a good night."

"Thank you, Ms. Maggie. I will. You do the same." She smiled and turned to head back to her cabin to dress for the captain's dinner. That was the table she, along with her parents, were expected to sit at every night they were on board. The captain knew them well and enjoyed having them around. She heard grumbling among the officers about being assigned to the captain's table and none of them seemed to enjoy it. But she loved it. She met a lot of interesting people having dinner with the captain and whichever officers were at his table that particular night. It made her feel quite grown up to sit with them and engage in interesting conversation with whomever she sat by, if she wasn't seated with her parents. For some reason, her brother got out of eating with them.

But Maggie did not decide to take the sailor training. She, her brother and her parents landed in Key West once on a vacation, months after that talk with the nice chief officer and they never wanted to leave. So, they stayed and after she graduated, she got her own little apartment facing the Gulf of Mexico. This was exactly where she wanted to be. She could still be near the sea and that was good enough for her. If she got the itch to be on it, she'd just book another cruise on that nice young officer's ship out of Miami or she'd hop on the catamaran and go to Dry Tortugas or on a sunset cruise. She didn't have to be working on whatever vessel she took. She just wanted to enjoy herself by being at sea as a passenger. And she surely did.

FOUR

When Maggie returned to her big white house on United, she rode her trike up the ramp as far as she could go and then walked it the rest of the way to her porch. She smiled when she saw the red shutters on all the windows. She'd had the contractor paint them to match her red trike. It was a decision she never regretted. Even if she'd had no trike, the red shutters were striking against the stark white of the house. The front door with the small stained glass window at the top was also bright red.

She was so proud of her big historic house on the corner of Duval and United. Before she won Powerball she rode past it time and again, always sighing because it wasn't her home. It really spoke to her and welcomed her, but it wasn't hers so it did no good to pine over it. Then that wonderful Saturday evening came when every one of her numbers were called. The first thing she did was ride past the house again and get the number of the real estate office that had it listed.

"You what?" Homer said to her when she told him. "You bought that big house on the corner? How? You don't have any relatives to leave you money and I know for a fact that you don't have any money of your own. You're just pulling my leg, right? This is your idea of a Saturday night joke?"

"Correction, Mr. Wiley, I didn't have any money before tonight."

He scratched his head, a sure sign of his confusion, and said, "Okay, I'll bite, Mag. What did you do? Raid the bank when you went in to cash a small check?"

"Nope. I won Powerball," she said as nonchalantly as she'd say, I got a chicken at Publix.

"You didn't!"

"I did! We're rich, Homer. We're filthy rich!"

"Oh my – you really won?" His grin was ear to ear and he couldn't have stopped smiling for any reason.

"I really won. Come on to my place. We have things to talk about."

"Hop on and I'll drive you over." His only means of transportation was, like with many locals, a moped, but no one on the island referred to them as mopeds, just scooters.

"No thanks, I'll meet you there," she said. She'd taken her life in her hands one time too many and nearly lost a leg when he jumped the curb to the sidewalk as a short cut to the Italian restaurant they both enjoyed. She swore then she'd never ride with him again and she walked all the way home from the restaurant.

"You're so stubborn. I would never let you get hurt on my scooter. You know that." The engine was idling and she was tempted but shook her head no, so he drove off to her place.

Around the kitchen table that night, over bottles of Sam Adams, Maggie told him she wanted him to work for her, now that she could afford him. First, she said, she wanted him to drive her to Miami to get a Hummer. He told her he'd be happy to do that, but that was no job and she said she was getting to that.

He took another big swig of the Sam Adams and waited. Maggie loved to be dramatic and draw things out. But he didn't have to be anywhere, so he just drank his beer and waited.

Finally, after she finished her third bottle, she told him. "I want you to be my chauffer."

He'd just taken another drink and when he opened his mouth, it came right back out and dribbled across the table. He hurried and grabbed a paper towel to stop it from going on the floor. "You want me to what?"

"You heard me. I'm serious. I'm tired of risking my life every time I need to get off this rock and go to the mainland. I really want you to drive me. I'll pay you $5000 a week, Homer."

His face blanched white and she thought he was going to pass out. He struggled so hard to keep himself afloat, playing his pipes and hustling to make ends meet in other ways, like diving for artifacts he could sell, and he deserved to make a decent living. When he could speak he said, "Maggie, I don't know what to say. $5000 a week! That's twenty grand a month!"

"Yes, it is. And it would be worth every penny to never have to drive again. I want you to start immediately. Let's leave tonight and go to a hotel until the car lots open in the morning." And that's how Homer came to work for her full-time. He was her chauffer, her body guard and always her friend.

"Hey, you two, I'm home. Carolyn, are you ready to go get some good grilled shrimp?"

"I'll be down in a jiffy," her friend told her from the landing of her third floor apartment Maggie'd had the contractor build for her with every convenience she could ask for in it.

"Homer," she said when she found him out on the back porch, "are you sure you don't want to go to dinner with us?"

"Nah, you two go ahead. I grabbed some grub at the bar with Lenny a half hour ago. I couldn't eat any more if I tried," he said with a big smile for her. "I'm going to be leaving in a couple minutes. Feel like calling it a night as soon as I reach Sugarloaf and my big old bed." She'd thrown a home on Sugarloaf in with the salary all those years ago to get him to work for her. He picked out one right on the water and loved it.

"Okay, but if you change your mind, you know where to find us. We'll probably grab a table outside, so that's where we'll be if you do decide to join us."

He came through the door into the kitchen, gave her a peck on the cheek, did the same to Carolyn as she passed him coming into the room, and told them both goodnight.

"I'm ready if you are, Mag," the other woman said, as she went out on the porch where Maggie had gone after Homer came into the house.

She was standing at the railing, looking over her big back yard. It was filled with every kind of tropical plant and tree the gardener could find for her, as she told him she wanted them all. The huge ficus tree's gnarled branches and roots took up a great deal of the left end of the expansive lawn. She was thinking about a night that might have ended with her losing her life right out there on the lawn across from the big tree, where Homer hid with his Glock and saved her life. She shivered, even though it was still in the low 80s outside.

"Let's go then," her friend told her. Even though Carolyn lived on the third floor of her home, they did not have a landlord/tenant relationship. Carolyn didn't pay her rent because Maggie said her home was a gift she wanted to share with her friends. Homer frequently stayed over and had his own room down the hall from Maggie. She'd already told Homer they were going to walk to the restaurant, so he said he'd see them at breakfast then.

~ ~ ~

"Maggie, please tell me you're not serious. That could get you killed and you know it."

"As serious as Mickey Lopez' heart attack last month." She swallowed the last bite of her grilled shrimp, as she looked out at the pale green water of the Gulf of Mexico from their table outside. "Ah, now that was a great grilled shrimp dinner."

"No, you don't get to change the subject on me. I can't let you do it. I just can't. If I have to get Homer, Lenny and everyone else in the KWPD to stop you, I'll do it. I will not sit idly by while you go play Spy Woman and get your head blown off by that maniac." She picked up her cup of tea with shaky hands, which her friend noticed. "Oh, wait a minute, what makes you think he's the one who's killing them, anyway? You have no proof, not a shred of evidence that points to him."

"It has to be him, Carolyn. No one really knows him or knew him before he landed his plane in Marathon and drove down here with his so-called medical license and set up shop. Have you ever been in that office?"

"Well, no, I've had no reason to go there, since I have my own doctor, Dr. Olson, just as you have. So, have you ever been in it and of course you have." She threw up her hands and shook her head back and forth.

"You're right. I have been in it. I went in and pretended I was searching for a dentist who did implants." That caused Carolyn to choke on the tea she'd just swallowed. Maggie stopped talking until her friend got control of herself and stopped coughing. Homer and Carolyn had been trying for years to get Maggie to go to Big Pine to see Dr. Troxel who said she had great bone and could have implants, but no way was this going to happen. She flat out refused every time it was mentioned. No durned ol' CIA was going to trace her by the microchips in those implants, she reminded them. "And, you ought to see that office. There are all kinds of magazines for people to read, including a medical magazine I've never heard of, scattered all over this huge low oblong table that takes up most of the room in the front office. And in the big back office where I thought there would be an office for him, one for a nurse, and examining rooms for patients . . ."

"You mean to say there are none of the above? Surely, that isn't what you're saying. The man's a doctor."

Maggie looked like she'd just licked the cream and said, "Is he?"

"Isn't he? Doesn't he have his medical diploma hanging in the outer office for his patients to see?"

"Nope. And as far as I could tell, by looking back into that big long room, there's none on the wall there, either. And I swear there are no exam rooms anywhere. And there's no nurse."

"But – what do you make of that, Mag? Did you see any patients there at all? And if so, what were they doing?"

"Well, while I waited for the young woman at the reception desk to get off the phone, I picked up a magazine and pretended to be looking through it, but I was really getting a good look at the rest of the office, that large room back of the waiting room partition. Yes, there was no wall, just a bunch of Japanese-screens. I forget what you call them, but you know what I mean."

"Yes, Shoji screens with washi paper."

"Yes, that's it. Shoji screens. There were about three of them I think separating the waiting room from the rest of the long hall of a room."

"Were there any people waiting?"

"One woman around thirty, I guess, was sitting there reading a Cosmopolitan magazine when I was standing there. She barely looked up when I walked in. I didn't recognize her. She was the only one."

"And no other patients in the place? That's really strange." Carolyn picked up her tea cup and took another sip, not coughing this time.

"No, there was one other patient."

Carolyn played with another piece of shrimp, trying to decide whether to finish it, since it was the only one left on her plate.

"Oh for goodness sakes, are you going to eat that or play with it?"

"Oh?" She smiled, and added, "No, I've had enough, so take it," and Maggie wasted no time in putting it on her own plate.

"Yes, he was in the back with Dr. Strangelove." She looked at Carolyn and grinned, getting a smile from her, too. "Anyway, he was sitting on a chair and Tobin was sitting in front of him and they were talking." She popped the grilled shrimp into her mouth.

"Was he taking his vitals or anything?"

"Nope, not that I could see. The doctor had on a white tee shirt so I could see there was no stethoscope around his neck and he had no lab coat on with pockets he could have put medical things in. There was no little table beside him where other instruments to check his eyes, ears, nose, and throat might be. Not even a little hammer instrument to check the patients' knee reflex, either."

"Oh my word, I wonder what he does with these people, if he doesn't examine them."

"That's what I tried to find out, but from what I could tell, all they were doing was talking."

"Did you see him leave?"

"No, the receptionist finally got off the phone. From the way she was talking I think it was a boyfriend she was speaking with and she didn't seem to mind that she was keeping a potential patient waiting. When she disconnected her cell phone, she looked up at me with a look that said 'why are you bothering me?'"

"Oh boy, that's not good."

"No, it sure isn't, but nothing about that whole setup is good. She finally spoke and asked if she could help me. I gave her the phony story about the implants and with no upper teeth, I expect it was easy for her to believe me."

"What did she say?"

Maggie laughed and said, "She said, 'Does this look like a dentist's office to you?'"

"And you said?" Carolyn was smiling, waiting for the good comeback she figured her friend would have.

"I said, 'Well, to be perfectly honest, this looks like a gym that's waiting for the basketball nets to arrive.'"

"You didn't? Oh my word, Mag!"

"Well, it's the truth, isn't it?" Her smile was mischievous. The waitress walked up to them to ask if they'd like more coffee and they both said yes, so she refilled their cups. They didn't want anything else at that moment, so after they thanked her, she left and Carolyn started talking again.

"What was her reaction?"

"She actually had the audacity to get all puffed up and huffy. She told me I needed to get out and look for a dentist elsewhere, that she needed to get back to work."

"So, you left."

"No, not yet," she said, laughing. "I asked her what kind of work she did."

"Oh, Maggie, no. You've let her know you think the whole doctor thing is phony. That might cause you a problem. Oh dear, I wish Homer were here."

"Why? There's nothing to do. I asked a legitimate question and had a good time watching her face darken with a burgundy hue. And then she said . . . she . . ." She couldn't finish for laughing again.

"What did she say that was so funny?"

"She said it was a . . . a doctor's office." She laughed and laughed at that and soon Carolyn was joining her, despite not wanting to laugh at the situation Maggie might have gotten herself into. "Can you believe that?"

"I hope you didn't laugh in the office."

"Well, I guess I kinda did, 'cause she called Dr. Tobin over, or rather he heard her raise her voice and came over to where we were." She started laughing again.

"Oh no, Mag. Now, you are in trouble."

"No, he was very nice or pretended to be, anyway. He asked what the problem was and before she could say anything, I told him I came in to ask the young lady whom I thought was an information desk person if she knew of a dentist in town who does implants. And I smiled really big at him. He didn't say anything for a minute and then he smiled and said something like, 'I'm pretty new in Key West, and I'm sorry but I don't know the name of one dentist, much less if any of them insert implants. I can see that you need them and it will be nice when you get your smile back. I'll bet it was a nice one.' Or words to that effect."

"He didn't! Was he being facetious or did you get the idea he was genuinely trying to be nice to you?"

"Oh, of course, he was being facetious. I just smiled at him, anyway, with my mouth that needs its smile back, and said, 'Well, I'm sorry I bothered you. I'll keep trying to find one who can help me and let you both get back to work,' except he'd just said he needed to get back to his patient, so I said I'll let you get back to - it.'"

"You are the epitome of everyone's worst nightmare," Carolyn said before she started laughing again. "And I'll bet you said that in a facetious tone, too."

"You'd win that bet if you'd put money on it. Yep, how could I be serious in saying I'd let them both get back to work. I mean what work was there? The man I thought was a patient might have been just a friend or maybe his boyfriend. Who knows? They were sitting knee to knee in there and he certainly wasn't examining him. He had nothing to examine him with, for goodness sakes."

"Still, what a chance you were taking by going in there pretending you were looking for a dentist's office." She wiped her mouth with the napkin and put it back on the table beside her empty plate. "Do you want dessert?"

"Is that a moon out there?"

Carolyn laughed and motioned for the waitress. "May we see a dessert menu, please?"

"Certainly." She reached in her large apron pocket and pulled out a slender three sided menu of desserts. "Here you go, ladies. Just let me know when you've made your decision," she said with a sweet smile.

"That chocolate mousse looks scrumptious, doesn't it."

"You read my mind," Maggie said. "That's exactly what I was thinking of getting."

Carolyn smiled at her friend and called the waitress back to their table, and she came right over.

"Decided, already?"

"Yes," Maggie told her. "We'd both like a big serving of that chocolate mousse."

The waitress laughed and said, "How did I know that's what you'd both want? I know you're locals and you're probably Key Lime pie'd out. Right?"

"It's still one of our favorites, but we like it when Maggie makes it."

"Well, Ms. Maggie, if you can make a better one than most of the places on the island, more power to you," she told them as she took back the menus and stuck them back in her pocket. "Chocolate mousse coming right up!"

"A gal after my own heart," Maggie said, before she turned to look at the moon. They were both quiet as they watched the clouds skim across it and the ribbons of satiny white shimmer on the water.

"That was fast," Carolyn said to the waitress who stood over them with the largest servings of chocolate mousse they'd ever seen. "And those are humongous!"

The waitress smiled and said, "We aim to please. Enjoy your mousse, ladies."

FIVE

"Over my dead body," Homer said, when Carolyn told him what Maggie wanted to do. "Have you finally lost your mind, Mag? You want to get killed for real this time? I won't be there to back you up again, you know." His glare was enough to destroy her, but she simply smiled at him.

"Oh, don't be so dramatic. You know I'll be fine. Besides, it isn't as though I'm going to sneak in there if he's there. I'm not that crazy."

"But why go near it, at all, and especially at night?" This time, Carolyn was truly frightened for her, even though they had no proof he'd killed anyone. "Please, just forget it. Let the police handle their investigation. If he's the killer, they'll get him."

Maggie continued to shuffle the deck of cards, as she'd been doing for the past five minutes since no one seemed eager to play the round of gin she'd proposed. They were too intent upon saving her life again, since she was bound and determined to risk it as she always did. She looked out one of the numerous kitchen windows at the egrets roaming around her big back yard. They were so close to the ocean that sea birds frequently found a place to search for tidbits of food in the big backyard.

"Maggie, did you hear me? I asked you to forget about it and leave it to Lenny and his team to find out who's committing these murders." Homer seemed more scared for her this time than all the other times when they were sure the guy was the killer. She wondered why, as she shuffled.

"Yes, I heard you. And I've no intention of interfering with Lenny's investigation. No one heard me say I was getting involved with it and I'm not."

"We didn't have to hear you say it, dear," Carolyn told her. "Everything you've said so far screams it loud and clear." She got up to get the three of them a cup of coffee since they weren't interested in another Sam Adams and she wasn't, either.

"None for me, Carolyn. Since we're getting nowhere with this one, I'm going in and watch the game. The Braves are killing it this season and I don't want to miss seeing them take the playoffs." He smiled at her, but had no smile for his beloved and exasperating Maggie.

"Wonder what's got his dander, tonight," she said after he'd left the kitchen.

"What? You know darned good and well what's got his – dander!"

"Carolyn, he's more upset about this – this fake doctor than the known killers I've – well - been involved with. Don't you think that's strange?"

"No, I don't. After all the times we've both faced horrible dangers with you, I just think Homer's reached his limit with them. I don't think he wants to deal with another murderous drama with you. Can't you see that?"

Maggie laughed, and took a sip of her tea. She didn't answer Carolyn.

"What? Nothing to say to that? What's so funny, anyway?"

"Homer and you. That's what's so funny. Why are the two of you even thinking about what I want to do? I think it's time you got lives of your own and leave mine alone."

"Why I never! Maggie Metronia, you've never talked to or about either of us like that before since I've known you and probably not since Homer has known you. Where do you get off telling us we need lives of our own?" She stood and went to the sink to rinse out her cup after dumping the tea out of it. "Goodnight!"

After she left, Maggie stopped shuffling the cards and spread a hand of solitaire for herself. She was glad both of them were gone. She could think better without all the prattle from them. This case was bothering her. This killer was too smooth and elusive. It wasn't that he was not in sight of the cops. It was that he was like southern molasses. Just way too slick for them. Like a magician of sorts. Maybe she was barking up the wrong tree, after all. Maybe that doctor whom she was certain was not a doctor was running a scam that had nothing to do with murder. Maybe he was just fleecing the ladies of their hard earned cash.

She surprised herself with that thinking. That was not how she operated. Even in her own head. She always was sure of herself and her opinion. She always was sure of her target. She knew when someone was guilty of murder. She just knew. She never had second thoughts. Well, admittedly she never had to have first thoughts, either. In the past, the killers just presented themselves to her in one way or the other. Like that awful Hamilton Jacques trying to push her out of the swing into the lake and into the mouth of an alligator! She shivered thinking of him. He almost sliced her head off right out there in her beautiful back yard a year ago after following them all to the island from West Palm Beach.

She got up and made another cup of tea. Tea always helped her to think clearly. And she had to think more clearly if she was going to find out what was going on in that place they called a doctor's office. Even if he was just running scams on unsuspecting women, he still needed to be stopped. And if he was doing worse to them, God knew he had to be stopped.

"I thought you and Carolyn were playing gin?" Homer reached in the fridge and got another beer.

"And I thought you were watching the baseball playoffs." She didn't look up at him, just kept playing solitaire.

"Your jack of clubs there," he said, reaching down to pick up the card, only to be swatted.

"I'll get there in my own time," she told him. "Go back to the TV."

"What's with you? And where's Carolyn?"

"Carolyn left in a huff and I'm concentrating – or trying to concentrate on my solitaire."

"Carolyn in a huff? What's that all about? Doesn't sound like her."

"Why don't you go ask her and leave me alone, okay?"

"Whoa! Something's sure got your goat tonight. And Carolyn in a huff? What the hell is going on in this house?"

"Get out, Homer. I don't want to have to throw you out of my kitchen. Just go and talk with Carolyn and leave me alone."

He bowed from the waist. "Yes, Ms. Garbo. Going now."

"Carolyn? Okay if I come in?" He was a little breathless from hurrying up the stairs.

"Sure, door's open."

She was sitting out on her terrace, staring into space. "Hey, what's going on around here? Did you and Maggie have a fight or something? Come on," he said, placing a hand on her arm as he sat in the matching wicker rocker. When she turned to him, he could tell she'd been crying. What the . . .

"What do you want, Homer?"

"Do I have to want something to visit you? Am I in the wrong house tonight or something? Everyone seems off key for some crazy reason."

"I'm sorry. I don't have to take it out on you, do I."

"I don't know. If I knew what 'it' was, maybe I could tell you, but no one wants to talk to me tonight. I know something's wrong between you and Maggie and for the life of me, I can't imagine what it is."

"You're right about that. Homer, she practically kicked me – and you – out tonight. If she'd told me to pack my things and get out, it wouldn't have surprised me."

"Maggie? You're talking about that little woman downstairs playing solitaire? That is the *she* you're talking about?"

She smiled and, as always, he felt a flutter when she did. He often wished he could find another woman to feel that way about, but he knew there'd never be another Carolyn for him. If only he could have this one.

"Yes, that Maggie. She said we both needed to get lives of our own and leave hers alone. And then she told me to get out of her kitchen. She always acted like it was 'our' kitchen, the three of us, even if I do have my own. And now, all of a sudden, it's her kitchen and she wanted me out of it in the worst way."

"There's something going on with her, that's for sure. She told me to get out, too, when I went in to get another beer to finish off the game. Personally, I think she's up to something she doesn't want our interference with. And if it's going after that phony doctor, it isn't good."

"What else can it be? That's all she's talked about for two or three days. That fake doctor and knowing he's the one who's been killing all those young women in these Keys. I'm really concerned for her this time, Homer. Usually she'll listen to us and this time she's having none of it. If we don't want to go with her, she'll go by herself and Lord knows what he'll do if he catches her spying on him. Maybe you should talk with the chief to let him know what's going on. Maybe they aren't even aware of this doctor. You know darn good and well he wouldn't want her interfering with another investigation, if they are or aren't thinking of this guy."

"I'll have a talk with her in the morning. Get some sleep, Caro," he said, as he planted a small kiss on her cheek.

"Good night, Homer. Hope your Braves win the game – the playoffs," she said with another killer watt smile for him.

"Thanks. Goodnight," he said as he hurried from her apartment. He knew if he stayed it might be different this time, at least on his part, and he didn't want to make a total fool of himself.

Six

"I don't know why I let you talk me into this. He's going to catch us, Mag!"

"Hush, he will if you keep talking. Let's be very quiet and try to hear what they're saying."

The man who called himself Dr. Tobin was standing behind a woman on a chair in the middle of the big room. He had on a sports coat that night, but no tie. They couldn't tell if he was wearing a tee shirt or dress shirt under it. She was dressed casually in a sun dress and flip flops. From the back, she looked fairly young, but they couldn't tell because she never turned around. They were talking too quietly for them to hear either one, and then the doctor reached over and turned off a floor fan after she pointed to it and hugged herself. It must have been blowing cold air straight at her.

"There, is that better?" They heard that clearly.

"Much, thank you, Dr. Tobin." She looked up at him and smiled. They could see she was barely out of her teens.

Then he started feeling around her neck. "Does your neck ever bother you?"

"No, it never has. Why?"

Before she got an answer, he took out a syringe with an extra-long needle on it and pushed the needle into the very top of her neck in back, and she said, "Ouch, that hurt. What did you d . . ."

He pushed her with one hand and she fell off the chair. "Goodbye, Ms. Kincaid."

"Oh my God, oh my God, Maggie, come on, hurry, we have to get out of here before he sees us looking in." She pulled Maggie away and they started running up the street toward their house. Before they reached it, they saw a police car coming toward them. Carolyn ran into the middle of United and waved him down.

"Lady, are you trying to get yourself killed?"

"Hurry, let us in, please, we're trying to keep from being killed," she choked out at him. Maggie had still not said a word since they saw him kill the young girl.

"I don't know what the two of you have gotten into this time, but sure, hop in the back. I'll drive a short piece away from here and you tell me, after I stop again, just what the hell you're running from that almost got you hit by a police car." He pulled away from United and got onto Simonton that ran parallel to Duval. He found a spot to park, and turned around in his seat. "Now talk."

"He killed her," Carolyn said. "Dr. Tobin killed a young woman."

"Wait a minute. You're saying Tobin, that young doctor who just came to town a few months ago, shot a young woman?"

"No, he didn't shoot her. He gave her something in a syringe in the back of her neck up high where it meets the skull. Just a few minutes ago. He asked her if her neck ever bothered her as he's feeling around it from in back of her, and she said no, and barely got it out when he jabbed a syringe with a long looking needle into her neck, and she tried to say what did you do, but could only get the first three words out when he took one hand, pushed her off her chair to the floor and said, 'Goodbye, Ms. Kincaid.' It was awful. Please, you've got to get some help and go to that office. We don't even know if she's alive. We just ran from the window and thank God you were coming down United. Had he heard us gasp out there, he might have come after us with the syringe next."

He was already on the radio calling it in and asking for backup. He waited as Lt. Butler told him to stay clear, until he sees another car coming toward him or the other way on United. He told him not to be a hero and burst into the office. He promised he wouldn't and waited, as did paramedics who'd just driven up near the building to go in when told it was safe for them. "Now, ladies, if you hear any shooting, I want you to get down to the floor mat as fast as you can go. Do I make myself clear?"

"Yes," Carolyn told him. Maggie just shook her head yes. Both women were learning that actually seeing a human being murdered was different from seeing the after-effects of a murder. They'd witnessed a killer being shot a year or so before, as he held a knife to her throat, but this was definitely different. "Maggie, are you okay?"

Again, Maggie just shook her head yes, that she was okay. Why did she have to get Carolyn and go to spy on that man who calls himself a doctor? He was no more a doctor than she was. He was using that title to lure unsuspecting women to that place to murder them. He must be the serial killer the police are searching for. He must kill them there and then take them to another place to throw off the police. As fast as her mind was going, she was unable to speak at that moment. She hadn't said a word since they witnessed the man who called himself a doctor murder the young woman in his office. She couldn't trust herself to open her mouth for fear of screaming at the top of her voice. And she couldn't understand that because she was never a screamer.

"Okay, ladies, just sit tight and do exactly what I said to do if you hear any shooting."

"All right, Sgt. Spivey, we will," Carolyn told him. At that moment, Homer came down the street toward them and she flagged him down. "On second thought, let us out so we can ride home with Homer. You can let us know when you want us to give our statements. I know you need them recorded to be legal."

"Good thinking," the sergeant said, "Hurry and get into the Hummer. Go home and stay there and we'll be in touch after this is all over. Go on, hurry."

They hurried to the Hummer where Homer was standing with the back door open, with a quizzical look upon his face. "What on earth have you two been up to that you were in the back seat of Spivey's squad car? I've been looking all over town for you, by the way. Where were you?"

"Just close the door, Homer, and get us home as fast as you can, please. We'll tell you everything as soon as we're safely home," Carolyn told him, her voice trembling now that the initial shock was over. Maggie still hadn't said a word.

"I can't leave you alone for a minute until you get mixed up in a crime of some kind. Did the perp who did whatever he did see you this time, too? I don't think any of us can go through months of waiting for him to come after the two of you like Jacques did Mag the last time."

"No, he didn't see us this time. Maggie, wait till Homer gets out before you get out." Homer had just parked the Hummer around the side of Maggie's big house on United and Duval, and when he got out, they both did, also, and hurried in front of him into the house.

"Sit, Maggie, I'm making us some tea," Carolyn ordered, as she got down the two cups and got a Sam Adams out of the fridge for Homer. As Homer and Maggie sat there, she filled the clear electric kettle with water and turned it on. They sat and watched it as it heated and then blue bubbles started churning in it. It was like her own Lava Lamp, Maggie had told them when she proudly showed them her latest purchase. As soon as it turned on, it lit up blue inside and was mesmerizing as all that blue bubbled up to the top.

Carolyn filled the two glass mugs with the tea after putting the peppermint teabags inside them. She and Maggie spooned their desired amount of stevia into the mugs and stirred it around with the small stirring spoons she got at the same time she bought the teapot. They just continued to stare at the water in their mugs until Homer broke their trance.

"Come on, out with it. You said you'd talk when we got home. Carolyn? Maggie? What happened that put you into the back of Spivey's patrol car?" He wasn't the world's most patient man under the best of times and now certainly was not the best of times and he knew it. He just knew it had something to do with murder.

SEVEN

"No! You didn't do that again! You both promised you'd never go sleuthing again no matter what! Oh my God in heaven, what am I going to do with the two of you? I really am considering taking you both to live in my place on Sugarloaf. You can't get into trouble there, because you'd not be in the city."

They'd never seen him pace like that before. He just kept moving and throwing his hands everywhere, while he was shouting at them. He never shouted at either of them before, either. They had to get him calmed down before he has a stroke or something.

"Okay, okay, Homer, try to calm down, please," Carolyn pleaded. "We didn't know we were going to be witnessing a possible murder. We just suspected he wasn't a doctor and wanted to see if he was with a patient and what he'd do. Dear God, never did we suspect what was going to happen. We just wanted to know if he'd pull out a stethoscope from somewhere and listen to a patient's chest or heartbeat. That poor woman."

Homer said nothing, just paced the floor after he'd yelled at them.

"I wish Spivey or someone would call so we'd know if she's still alive," Carolyn said to no one in particular.

I do, too, Maggie was thinking, but I have a feeling we're not going to get that news.

Homer was out on Maggie's back porch. They watched as he still paced one way and then the other. That wasn't like him. He couldn't really be thinking of moving them to Sugarloaf. Surely not. They were both thinking the same thing.

Maggie got busy in the kitchen. She opened the freezer door and took out an apple and Key lime pie. Might as well have them ready for all of them when Spivey or whoever else shows up. She turned on the oven and set it to the temperature she wanted and then put the apple pie in it. She set the Key lime in the pie holder on the counter so it could begin to defrost. She knew she should do it in the fridge but there wasn't that much time.

As it turned out, no one came to the house. Sergeant Spivey called them, instead. "Why don't you ladies come to the station around ten tomorrow."

"Has something happened? Did you find the woman?"

"No, the chief just said it would be better if you came in tomorrow, since it's late."

"Yes, yes, we can be there. Ten sharp. I'm so afraid you're going to be too late, that you'll find the woman dead. I wish now we'd broken in somehow. Maybe we could have stopped him. Yeah, I suppose you're right. Okay, we'll see you in the morning. Nite."

"Look, Carolyn, we heard what you told Spivey, and I want you to sit down with Maggie right now."

"Why? What's wrong?" She was easing down into a chair around the kitchen table.

"Wrong? Oh nothing, except I think Maggie's wearing off onto you. You wish you'd broken in? That monster is a serial killer, and you wish the two of you could have broken in to save that woman? He would have killed all three of you. Don't you get it? He's killed multiple women who've been found all over the Keys. At least, they probably think he's good for it now, after what you witnessed. He wouldn't have hesitated to immobilize the two of you, too, and then the police would have three victims in the morgue instead of the one they're probably going to have before the night's over."

Biting her lip, she said, "I'm sorry. I wasn't thinking when I said that. It was just the thought that they'd get there too late to save her from dying."

He turned and leaned against the railing, almost afraid to open his mouth again. He wanted to drill the fear of God into them. He wanted to scream at both of them and keep screaming at both of them until they got into the Hummer and went to Sugarloaf with him.

"Homer?" No response. "Please come in and sit down. I have a Sam Adams opened for you. Let's all talk rationally," Maggie told him. It was the first she'd spoken since it happened.

"Rationally? Nothing about this is rational. I think she meant it when she told Butler she wishes the two of you had broken in and stopped that maniac. And I'm sure you were chomping at the bit to get inside there – again. Only this time illegally."

"Please sit down. We can't have a conversation with you pacing like that."

Finally, without a word, he sat down and took a long swig of his beer and said, "Thank you."

"We know it isn't rational. It isn't every day the two of us watch someone deliberately end someone else's life, you know? This has been really hard for both of us, but you have to know we didn't want to find out anything except what he did with his patients, since I didn't see anything resembling an exam room or medical supplies in there. That's all, really." She took a big drink of the coffee she forgot she'd poured. It wasn't hot but still warm.

"Yes, she's right. I was telling the truth, Homer. Haven't you ever heard anyone or for that matter, haven't you, yourself, ever played the "if only" game out of guilt, thinking there surely would have been something you could have done to prevent this or that if only – fill in the blanks."

He scratched his head, something he always did when he was confused or not understanding what was going on. He took another drink of the Sam Adams, but didn't react one way or the other, didn't say a word.

"Well, haven't you?" Maggie asked.

Finally, he said, "Okay, I understand, and of course, I've played the "if only" game with myself. Sorry, I freaked out on the two of you. I just couldn't believe, after all we've been through together because of your getting involved in a murder case, that not one, but both of you were out getting involved in this one."

"And we've said we're sorry." Carolyn still felt so shaky she could barely hold the cup of tea she'd made for herself after Homer came in and sat down.

"I know you did, but how many times has Mag promised us both no more getting curious and investigating for herself. Only this time she got you to go along with it," he said, with a raised voice again. "Why, Carolyn? Why would you go along with her instead of stopping her as you always tried to do? That's what I don't understand." He was on his feet again, his hands flying around faster than an Italian mother.

She stood and faced him. "I don't know why I went along with her. Okay? I was scared for her, afraid he'd catch her spying on him and report her to the police or something. I certainly did not think he'd hurt her or hurt me if I went with her. Or that he'd end up murdering an innocent young woman in front of our eyes!"

"Yes, neither of us thought anything would happen. I just suspected he wasn't a real doctor and wanted to see what he did with people who came to him – I mean, did he sit them down and counsel them, give them a massage – I just had to see for myself what someone with no real medical supplies or exam room did when a patient came to his office. And why at night when it was dark in the lobby area? But murder? Dear God, no. That was the furthest thing from my mind. It never even entered my mind, period."

The house phone rang again and Carolyn spilled her tea getting up to answer it. "I, sure, we're still up." She looked at the phone, and then turned to them but said nothing.

"Well?"

"What was that all about?" Maggie knew it had to be the police.

"That was odd."

"What was odd? Come on, tell us what he said," Homer said to her. "It was Butler, not Spivey, wasn't it."

She nodded. "He just asked if we were all up and you heard me tell him we were. And he just said they're on the way over and that was it. He hung up before I could ask him anything."

"Sounds like cryptic Butler. Always creating drama." Homer's connection to the lieutenant went way back to their teen years when even in school they never got along. He tolerated the guy but that was the extent of it. Most days he'd just as soon get him in the ring and battle it out as look at him.

Maggie smiled at him. "When are the two of you going to grow up and forget that you don't like each other very much, if that's even a true statement?"

He looked up and shot her a look, but didn't say anything. She knew why it wouldn't happen. They were both too durned stubborn to admit it or apologize and let it go.

He was tending to the grill after their dinner, as it was his domain and no one else touched it, unless it was to grill something. He was the one who kept it shining like new.

"Butler's car just pulled up on United. I wonder why it didn't sound like this is going to be a good meeting between them and us. What could have happened, except they're angry about the sleuthing, when we promised it wouldn't happen again, Maggie?" She smiled when she said it. She couldn't really get angry with her friend, much less stay angry with her if she ever did feel that way.

All of a sudden, the chief was in the room, Butler behind him. "Okay, you two. Start talking and tell me why you sent us on a wild goose chase," Doan wasn't playing. He was truly angry and he rarely got angry with Maggie. He and Butler sat down at the table and refused a piece of the apple pie Maggie held out to them. They always had a piece of her pie, whether it was apple, peach, cherry or Key Lime, but the apple Maggie made melted in their mouths and they could never turn it down. Now they were all business. There would be no pie this time, and Maggie sensed it and wasn't sure what he wanted her to say.

"I don't understand, Chief. Why do you say it was a wild goose chase?" Carolyn was as puzzled as Maggie. She sipped her tea with her elbows on the table, as she looked over her soothing cup at Doan.

"Because you made the whole thing up, that's why." He got up and walked to the counter to pour a cup of coffee that Maggie had just put into the percolator. He watched as it perked and bubbled up into the clear plastic top, and grabbed a cup as soon as it stopped. "Anyone else want one while I'm up?" Butler said he'd like one, but the rest of them sat still, not saying another word. When he sat back down, he glared at the women.

"Okay, Chief, this has gone far enough," Homer said. "You know as well as I that if they said they saw a guy murder a woman or try to, since they don't know if she's still alive, then by damn, that's what happened." He got up and went out on the porch, his fingers clenched tightly on the rails as he looked out at the blackness of the sky and its myriad stars. Usually, with the street lights and other bright lights, they were obscured but tonight he saw a whole sky full of them. That sight always calmed him when he was home on Sugarloaf Key and tonight was no different. He didn't want to lose his temper to the extent he'd end up hitting one or both of them until they came to their senses and admitted that Maggie and Carolyn wouldn't lie about something this important.

The chief stared down into his cup, and then he looked up at them again, this time with less hostility. "Ladies, we had a long chat with your "pseudo" doctor a few minutes ago right before Butler called to say we were on our way over."

"And?" Maggie was staring him right in the eye, this man she used to baby-sit when he was a boy. Nothing shy about him then, as he used the whole island and mostly its surrounding seas as his playground, as did all the conch children who grew up there. He was a hard one to keep in check until his mother got home, but Maggie managed to do it, even if it meant she ended up sitting in the sand on the beach watching him surf with his friends, if the waves were high.

Doan looked away for a moment, listening to the gulls out on the water. There must have been a hundred of them in the one spot when he and Butler drove up to United and parked in their usual spot on the side nearest Maggie's big white house. Seemingly calmer, he turned back to her. With a steady non-combative voice, he said, "There is no body.

We looked in every corner and under every piece of furniture in the place. No woman was lying injured or dead in that building."

Both women gasped and Carolyn told him again, "Chief, we were at that window for at least twenty minutes. One minute he's talking with the young woman who sat on the chair in front of him, asked her if anyone has ever messed with that part of her neck he had his hands on. He'd been gently massaging the upper part of it where it meets her hairline. And then as quick as taking a breath, he plunged a syringe with a very long needle down into that spot. She asked, "What . . . what did you. . ."

Maggie added, "She never finished that sentence and he nudged her off the chair with one hand, saying, "Goodbye, Ms. Kincaid."

Butler's head snapped up. "You're sure he called her Ms. Kincaid?"

She fidgeted in her chair and nodded in the affirmative, hoping this time they believed her. Lenny'd known her practically his whole life and surely he knew by now that she might be curious and she might get into some bad messes because of it, but she would never lie, especially about something this serious.

Doan sat quietly for quite a while, staring out at the swaying palms that filled Maggie's back yard, along with the giant ficus where Homer hid among its gigantic roots more than a year ago, with his Glock trained on the killer who held a knife to her throat, until she saw him and took his unspoken advice to pretend to faint. As she fell back toward Hamilton Jacques as he motioned for her to do, so the knife wouldn't plunge into her neck before she slid to the ground, he took his shot as did the KWPD sniper who'd come running from across the street from where he and his partner were hiding in the Southernmost Motel. Carolyn, who'd been watching in horror from her terrace, called him. His shot to the head was the one that put an end to the killer who'd followed Maggie and Carolyn to Key West from West Palm Beach, where Maggie had witnessed him discarding parts of a body in the compactor. Doan sighed, remembering how close they came to losing Maggie Metronia that night.

He looked back at her and said, "We had a report a couple hours ago from a father who said his daughter, Lily Kincaid, was supposed to come to dinner early this evening at his home and she never showed. He said she never missed dinner with him and his wife, because he has terminal cancer and she wanted to spend every moment with him on her evenings off from the library. We told him we couldn't really do anything officially for a few more hours but we'd be on the lookout for her. He gave me a photo of her." He handed the photo to Maggie.

"That's her," they both said, looking sadly at the image of the lovely young woman, before handing it back to the chief.

Doan looked at Butler and they stood from Maggie's table where, at some point in their questioning of Maggie and Carolyn, there had appeared small dishes of the apple pie they'd refused and fresh cups of coffee, both of which they automatically had indulged themselves in as they had dozens of times before.

"We'll let you know when we find Ms. Kincaid, ladies. Thanks for the pie and coffee," Butler said, before they went through the kitchen door to the porch to take the stairs down to the backyard near their car.

"You believe us, then?" Maggie said, absently twisting the bottom of her cotton top, as was her habit when she was anxious about something.

Doan smiled a tired smile and said, "Yes, Mag, we believe you. Now, unless you want Homer to take you home to Sugarloaf Key, you'll stay put and let us find the young lady you witnessed being murdered – if that's the outcome of the needle in her neck."

"We'll stay right here, Chief," Carolyn assured him, as she started to clear the dishes.

"Mag?" Doan wanted to hear it from her own lips as she had a way of being non-committal by not saying anything, and then they'd catch her out sleuthing on her own.

"Okay, I don't want to run into that guy, so sure, we'll both stay right here. Please let us . . ."

"I'll call you as soon as we know anything. Homer, you know what to do," he admonished.

"Don't worry, they aren't going anywhere." He walked the two officers out to the porch and asked, "Do you think he saw them?"

"No," Doan told him. "They both said they backed away from the window and started running as soon as she fell off the chair and that the phony doc didn't look in their direction. I'm sure he didn't know anyone saw what he did."

"That's a relief. We don't need a killer looking for Maggie – and Carolyn – again. We've had more than enough of that terror. 'Night, Chief. Butler."

EiGHT

They told him goodnight and went down the stairs and to their car. "Well, Blake, I guess we'd better pick him up again. It's going to be a hell of a long night."

"Yeah, I guess it is. He's so cagey I can't see him telling us a thing. He'll probably bring along a lawyer this time."

"I fully expect that," his boss told him. "He'll clam up with the help of the best lawyer he can find in South Florida."

Before they got to the home of the doctor, there was a call over the radio - another body of a young woman, like the others, found lying by the water on the beach. Smathers, this time. They turned the car around and headed that way.

"Well, Spivey?"

"Duplicate of the other two, Chief," the sergeant told him when he walked up to the scene. "Just lying there, fully dressed, like she was sleeping. No visible wounds on her."

"ID?"

"Nope, nothing near the body."

Doan took out the photograph of Lily Kincaid and walked with Butler to the body. "No doubt who this is. Poor girl."

"You know her?" Spivey asked.

"No, but her parents put in a missing report tonight on her. She's the one Maggie and Carolyn saw that so-called doctor kill. Come on,

Butler." He looked back at the sergeant and said, "Tell Doc to check the base of her skull for a needle mark. For once I'm glad those two weren't minding their own business. Let's make the notification and then we'll pick him up."

It only took them a couple minutes to get to the Kincaid home on AIA, not far from where their daughter was found. When they walked up on the porch, the light came on and the door opened. There stood Rose Kincaid, fastening her robe tightly about her waist. Her face was pale as a sheet of paper. Her husband John came up behind her, also tying the robe he'd thrown over his pajamas when he heard the car stop in front of the house.

"Did you find our Lily?" he said, since his wife was starting to cry.

"May we come in, please?" Doan asked, hesitantly.

"Where are my manners," Rose managed to say," yes, please, come inside."

John showed them to the living room and motioned for them to take the two chairs opposite the plaid covered sofa. He pulled his wife gently down beside him.

"I'm so sorry to have to tell you . . ."

Lily's mother's keening was soft at first and then became a loud scream that seemed to the officers to continue for fifteen minutes, though it was probably fifteen seconds, and then she started to sob quietly into her husband's shoulder. He held her tightly to him and said, "How? Where? Where did you find her?"

Doan hated to tell them she was found on the beach almost across the street from them, but he couldn't lie. "She was found lying on the beach."

"Which beach?" John asked, though he seemed to know.

He hesitated, before saying "Smathers."

"What!" his wife screamed out. "Our beach? She was found across the street?"

"It was a little piece down the street, but yes, it was across the street from you."

"Oh God, John, she was lying there the whole time and we didn't know it. We didn't know to go help her."

"Ms. Kincaid, there was nothing you could have done even if you'd found her. She'd been – gone a while before our officers found her. No one could have done anything. I'm so sorry."

"Oh God. Oh God, my baby, oh God, Lily."

"How did she look, Chief? Was she hurt badly before he did what he did to – to kill her?" John was trying to stay calm so he'd understand everything they had to say, but he was screaming inside.

"She was fully dressed and there were no apparent injuries, but the medical examiner will check her carefully when she gets her in a little while, if they haven't taken her already."

"She's still there? Lying on the beach? Our little girl's still lying there?"

"They were getting ready to take her to the medical examiner when we left."

"How can you be sure? John, I want to go to her – now. Let's go."

"We'll need you to identify her when the medical examiner is ready," Doan told her. "She wouldn't be on the beach now."

"You don't know that. John, let's go," she insisted, pulling him off the couch. "I want to see my daughter now."

"We'll take you to her," Butler said, shrugging inconspicuously at Doan. He knew there was no way she was not going to that beach, with them or without them.

"Thank you Lieutenant," John told him, as they went out the door. "We appreciate this." They didn't bother getting into street clothes.

When they got into the back of the car, Doan said, "We'll drive by the scene, but I'm sure she's been taken to the medical examiner's office by now. Do you want to go there?"

"Yes, please," her father said, "if she isn't – isn't on the beach, please take us to – to where they took her." His voice broke then, "You said we'd have to do the ID, anyway, right?"

"Yes, you will have to at some point."

"Then, we'll do it now," Rose Kincaid said, her voice weak from sobbing. "We'll go see our little girl. She never hurt anyone in her life, you know," and then she started crying again.

They drove past the scene, slowly, seeing that what they told the Kincaids was true, their daughter had already been taken. The only ones still on the beach were the officers working the scene and what looked like a hundred seagulls, all screaming for food from the ocean, as one by one, they dived into it. At the scene, it was obvious they weren't going to find anything. Tobin had made sure of that, Doan thought as they passed.

Seeing the yellow crime scene tape, John asked, "Was that the place, Chief?"

"Yes, that's where she was found. Again, I'm very sorry for what you're going through. What your daughter went through, although we don't think she suffered. We think it was very fast."

"What was very fast?" Rose's voice was louder now. "Do you know something you're not telling us? Do you know how our daughter died?"

"I - I don't know anything for sure, but we are going by the condition she was in. We could see no visible bruises or other marks on her. That's usually a sign there was no struggle."

"She wasn't shot or – or stabbed?"

"No, Mr. Kincaid, we're sure she wasn't shot or stabbed."

"And you said she was fully clothed, too?"

"Yes, ma'am, she was fully clothed and nothing seemed to have been disturbed."

"You mean she wasn't raped, right?" John said.

"It looks that way, but until the medical examiner does the – the exam – we won't know for sure what happened to your daughter. We're here. We'll take you to the office."

"You can say morgue, Chief. We know they have to do an autopsy to find out what happened to our Lily. No need to treat us with kid gloves. We know what has to be done," Rose told him, before she started to sob again, as they walked into the building. She was almost collapsing by then, and suddenly shaking all over, not an unusual reaction when a loved one is nearing the morgue and the dead body of that one who meant the world to them. Her husband was having a difficult time walking her into the building where their lives would change forever.

Doan started to help but he motioned him away with a shake of his head. They would face it together, without any help.

When they got to the window, the curtain was drawn. Doan picked up the phone and the curtain was pulled apart. In front of it was a litter and on the litter was the still clothed body of the daughter they loved so much. Rose Kincaid sobbed louder then and her husband said, almost in a whisper so low the two officers barely caught it, "I'm dying. I was supposed to go first, then Rose, and then our Lily. That's the order of things. This is just wrong. It's all so wrong," he said, louder, before turning into his wife's arms and sobbing, too.

"I want to go in. I want to be next to my daughter," Rose said, suddenly.

"I don't know if you should, Ma'am," Butler told her. "Your – Lily won't feel the same to you. She was lying out there for . . ."

"I don't care about that. I just have to go in there to be with her. Can't you understand that?"

"Please," her husband said, "Rose is right. We have to go to our daughter."

Doan got on the phone again and they saw someone pick it up. Then the door opened and Butler motioned them in. He and Doan stayed in the hallway as the two of them went in to their daughter.

"She's so cold – and – and almost hard, John," his wife said as she sobbed. Still, she leaned over the table and held her daughter in her arms. "I'm so sorry, baby girl. Mommy's so sorry." It was a hard scene to watch, but not one the seasoned cops had not seen before many times. To say they never got used to it would be an understatement. It was impossible to get used to it.

After several minutes of both of them clinging to the cold dead body of their daughter, John said, "Rose, honey, it's time to go and let them take care of her. They have to find out what was done to our little girl."

"Oh John, I don't want to leave her. She'll be all alone." She lay her upper body across hers and sobbed again loudly. There were no more bodies in the morgue at the time, so the doctor and her staff were in no hurry. They tried to be as unobtrusive as possible with the couple. Finally, Rose raised up and said, "I'm ready to go. Lily, we'll – we'll –

oh God – this is so awful. You've been our world since the day you were born and you'll always be with us. We love you, baby girl. Daddy will – Daddy will be with you – be with you soon, so you won't be alone and I'll see you as soon as I can. Sleep in peace till then, sweet girl. Love you." She planted a kiss on her daughter's lips, her husband leaned down and kissed her dry cold cheek and then they turned away, murmuring their thanks to the doctor and her staff for letting them tell her goodbye.

It was about as emotional a scene as they'd seen in there for a very long time and although they tried to harden themselves against any feelings of anything except empathy for the families, they admitted that this one was hard. Seeing that the parents did not look back through the window before being escorted away by the chief and Butler, one of the assistants closed the curtain and wheeled Lily Kincaid over to the table. The doctor was ready to begin, as soon as she undressed the deceased.

NINE

"Do you remember which house it was, Butler?"

"I know it was bright yellow with green shutters. It had recently been painted. It used to be a dingy white."

"I have it. 405. Okay, let's roll," he said, eager to arrest the phony doctor as quickly as possible.

They pulled up in front of the house and noticed all the lights in the house were on, unusual these days when everyone was conscious of climate change and turned out lights in rooms they were not using right then. They couldn't be in all the rooms, so why all the lights at this late hour?

"Is that a red trike at the other side of the street? Dear God, no! Maggie! Come here!" he hissed in a whisper, but she heard it loud and clear.

She came out from behind a large ficus tree, reluctantly. "Good job, Mag. You sure know how to stay put when you promise you will." He kept his voice down, but couldn't hide the exasperation in it.

"I'm sorry, Chief. I just didn't want him to take off before you got here. I was just riding the trike around the bay to relax myself, since I couldn't sleep, and when I got to Smathers, I saw the crime scene tape on the beach so I rode over here. Figured you hadn't made it to his house yet with a scene to work. It's her, isn't it? It's Ms. Kincaid."

"Yes, I'm sorry to say it is Lily Kincaid. But that doesn't excuse you. Now I want you to get back on that trike of yours and head for home while we do our job and get this guy arrested. Maybe then, the young women down here can feel safe, again."

"Okay, I'll get out of your hair. He's still in there. I saw him pacing around in a room in the middle of the house – on that side."

"Thanks, *Ms. Marple*. Now, may we get to work?" Doan half-grinned at her and she gave him a big toothless smile, got back on her trike, waved and left.

"Now that that's taken care of, I'll call for backup and we'll get this guy taken down," Butler told his boss, who nodded, as he was putting on his vest. Butler'd put his on while Doan was talking with Maggie.

Several officers drove up without lights or sirens, as they were told to do. They all piled out of the cars and went to Doan and Butler, for their instructions. Two men took each side of the large house. Doan, Butler, and another officer with a battering ram took the north side, since that's where Maggie saw Tobin pacing. They saw him in the windowed family room. He was alone. Their research of him revealed no family in Florida. There was an ex-wife and two college-age children in the Smokies in north Tennessee. So far, with all the lights on, he hadn't seen them or noticed anyone else around the house, so supposed they were still up north.

They looked for a door to breach, and when they found it, Doan signaled the officer to ram it when it didn't open. The phony doctor was startled, but took off running for the front of the house. Doan tackled him, almost got a good hold on him, but he kicked him in the face and got away from him. "What the – the jerk sprayed cooking grease all over his clothes," one of the men shouted. None of them could get a good hold on him, including two at the front door who tried to stop him.

It was so dark that at first they couldn't see where he went, and then Doan shouted, "The boat!" They all started running for the dock, but the boat left it as soon they got there. One of them stumbled over a red trike, and told the chief about it.

"No! I don't know how she managed it, but Maggie's on that boat with him!"

"What in hell does she think she's going to accomplish? She has no weapon and that guy's just gonna kick her overboard first chance he gets, chief," Spivey said. "At least, I don't think she carries."

"No, she doesn't and right now I'm sorry about that. The boat should be here in a couple minutes, so we'll just have to try to get a couple men on board to take him down," Doan told him. "Let's just hope Mag stays out of sight until that happens. Surely she knew we'd be shooting at him on the boat and now we don't dare risk it until we get close to it. I've half a notion to arrest her for obstruction this time, when we get her safely off that boat. Maybe that'll teach her not to interfere."

"Fat chance, Chief. Maggie will always be a wannabe sleuth!" Butler told him, with a grin. Some of the guys snickered. "You can take the freedom from the woman, but you can't ever take the sleuth out of 'er. You've certainly given it your best shot these past few years."

"You're right, but she deserves to be scared this time – if she lives through it, that is. If he spots her before our guys get on that boat, that's all she wrote for Maggie. He'll throw her in the water so fast she won't know what hit her. And this time, we probably won't be able to save her as dark as it is tonight! Where's – oh there it is. Okay, let's all pile on the boat. Spivey, you and Oates jump on his, as soon as we catch up with him. Some of us will slip aboard after we're sure he hasn't seen you. Or if he has and starts shooting."

"You got it, Chief. We're all set." They went to port side to wait till the police boat could catch up with his. They never planned for their night to include hopping into a killer's boat, but then who plans any night when one's a cop. They have no control over what those eight hours or more are going to bring. Most nights in Key West are so quiet they get to walk the streets and enjoy conversations with the locals and the tourists if they're sober enough to carry on a conversation, since so many start drinking as soon as the bars open in the morning. Other nights are like this, especially when they have a serial killer on the loose and no one has an inkling of an idea who and where he can be and when he's going to strike again. Well, they all knew who and where this one was and if the two of them have anything to say about it, he's struck for the last time.

Maggie was hiding in the stern of Tobin's boat, well away from the gunwale and out of sight. She sure didn't want to go overboard again as she had in the Straits a couple years ago. She had no memory of it, but was told it was hard for Homer to find her and the waters look even darker tonight. She had no idea why she suddenly ran ahead of him to hide in his boat. Sometimes it just feels right to do something, only now that she was on the boat alone with him, she had no idea what she'd intended to do. If she even thought about it before she ran for it. All she knew now was that that she was there and he was there, she was so terrified she could barely think. He must hear her heart pounding clear up in the bow of the boat.

Tobin was several feet from Maggie, steering the boat. He thought for a minute he saw another boat closing in on him but it must have been his imagination, because his looks in the mirror revealed a clear sea free of the lights of other water craft. That was good because he didn't want to have to deal with other boats right now. He just wanted to get as far away from these ridiculous Keys as he could get tonight before it gets too dark to see anything. His external lights were off, as he didn't want to attract attention. So far it didn't look like they were able to follow him, although he was aware of their water patrol unit, having watched them at work. Now, there was a bit of light on the water from the sliver of a crescent moon, so right now it would have to do in place of his boat lights.

What was that? He could have sworn he heard a sneeze, but he'd looked over the boat when he got on board. Granted it was just a cursory search but it wasn't like his boat was large with a lot of hiding places. There was no galley, no sleeping area, no nothing except what a person saw on the surface of the boat. He liked it that way. When he'd needed to sleep in the past, he just piled some quilts on the bench in the stern and went to sleep. He had a little fridge where he kept plenty of beer stocked and any sandwich fixings if he was going to be out fishing for a while. Of course, he wasn't sure he'd have to take the boat out tonight, but he'd stashed a little food in it early in the day, just in case.

Spraying that vegetable oil all over his white shirt and pants was a prince of an idea, if he did say so himself. It made him so slick that even that giant of a cop couldn't hold him. Butler, he thought his name was. He laughed aloud at that. When he felt safe enough to stop after he got well away from the Florida Keys, he'd change clothes, but right now he had to concentrate on getting away.

As they caught up to his starboard side, both men jumped the gunwale and landed just inches from where Maggie was hiding. "What the hell?" they all heard Tobin yell. All of a sudden, a shot rang out from the bow of the boat that was now spinning out of control as he had to forget about the wheel and concentrate on getting rid of these cops who were hell-bent upon taking him prisoner. Not going to happen in this lifetime.

Maggie knew even if he didn't kill them, they were all going to die anyway from the boat crashing. She was scared to death of boats. They were so long from bow to stern, she'd never in her life tried to steer one for fear she'd tear it up. But who else was there. She didn't want to die from a boat explosion and she was sure that would happen if it collided with the police boat. She took a deep breath and while he was occupied with his gun, she risked inching further toward the bow, so she could grab the wheel, since they were now spinning in a circle and nearly collided once already with the police boat.

Tobin didn't seem to notice and ducked as a shot from Spivey came close to his head. With the noise of all the shooting from both sides, Maggie was able to get to the bow and take the wheel. By damn, despite never steering a boat in her entire life, she was going to steer this one. She was not about to die out there on the almost pitch black ocean if she could help it. At first she did no good at all. The boat just kept spinning in circles. She fell once but managed to get up and get back to the wheel. She held tight to it and with all her might, despite weighing just 100 pounds, she was able to start correcting.

Realizing she'd managed to straighten up the boat, Doan and Butler jumped into it, and Butler ducked as Tobin's shots were directed toward them now. Doan wanted to get to Maggie before that phony realized she'd taken over control of his boat and started shooting at her, too, like the fool he was, even though she was saving all their lives by her quick and courageous action.

He crawled on his belly toward the bow that seemed the length of three football fields to him in his anxiety about reaching her in time. Tobin must have heard him, because a spray of shots came very low and close to where he'd just been.

"Hey, Doc, look this way," Butler yelled to him. Tobin ducked behind a large crate, spraying more rounds at the three of them as he did.

"You'll never take me," he shouted over the sound of the engine.

"Just answer one question," Butler yelled in response. "Why? Why did you kill all those young women? They never hurt a soul and they certainly never hurt you. They went to you for help."

The fake doctor laughed and said, "It wasn't about them hurting anyone."

"Then, why?" he repeated. "Why did you do it?"

"Mostly because I could," he said, spraying them again.

Doan finally reached the bow and grabbed the wheel from Maggie, who started to scream, but he put his other hand over her mouth. "It's me, Maggie. Don't scream. I don't want him to see you."

"Lenny?"

"Yes, it's me. I'll take over. You get down and lie still until I tell you to get back up."

"But I'm doing a good job here. You go help the guys."

"That wasn't a request, Mag. Now get down on the damned deck."

Hearing that tone of his voice that she'd never heard very often, Maggie did as he instructed, while he steered the boat toward Key West and the police dock, behind the police boat that was not getting too far ahead of him, since there was no way to know how this was going to finish or when the guys might jump back in, or at least throw Maggie into it.

Finally, Oates, the officer Spivey came aboard with, managed to get behind Tobin and soon the man felt a gun at his head. "It's over, Tobin. No one's gonna shoot, if you lay down your weapon," Butler yelled to no avail as another round almost got Spivey and him both, before he tackled him, as Oates, a former Navy Seal, reached up and grabbed the weapon from him. Spivey rushed him, too, as Butler threw the cuffs on him. "I told you it was over."

Tobin smiled and said, "We'll see about that. Tell your goon to get the metal off my hands."

Butler ignored him and Spivey put cuffs on his ankles. "Hey, that hurts. Get it off me. It's too small." This time Spivey laughed and read him his rights. Oates went to the bow to ask the chief if he wanted him to steer the boat to the dock, and was told yes.

"What about me?" Maggie started to stand up, but before she could, Doan slapped a cuff on one wrist. "What are you doing? If it weren't for me, you'd all have drowned because the boat woulda crashed into yours." The chief ignored her and pulled her up, putting the other wrist in the other cuff.

"Maggie Metronia, you are under arrest for obstructing law enforcement in the apprehension of a wanted murderer. You have the right to remain silent. Anything you say can and will be held against you in a court of law. Do you understand?" She nodded yes, and then he walked off, leaving her standing there with her toothless mouth open, but silent. Doan turned around and helped her over to a seat. "Sit there until we get to the dock so you won't fall."

Maggie was too shocked and angry to say another word. How dare that young whippersnapper do this to her, of all people. The ungrateful little – oh, what's the use, what's done is done. Homer will take care of him in record time. Had she known this was the way he'd repay all her kindness when she baby-sat him, she'd have never let him go to the ocean to surf when he was supposed to be home doing his homework until his parents got home.

She seethed all the way to the dock. There was a crowd waiting since several people saw what was going down off shore. Someone had even called that photographer Rob O'Neal from *The Citizen*, and he was taking pictures of her along with that killer. As though she were a criminal, too. And, oh my God, there's Mandy Miles, that star reporter for the Keys Weekly, probably planning to make this front page news.

"Hey, Maggie, what's going on?" Miles called to her from the shore, as O'Neal kept snapping those pictures of her. "Why are you in cuffs? Did you help this guy? Is he a real doctor? Did he kill those women?" She could already see the headlines, "Bone Island Maggie arrested with serial killer." She'd always liked Maggie, but loved the thought of that headline above her story.

Maggie wasn't about to say a word. She wasn't talking to anyone but Homer. Where was he? He always knew what was going on before anyone else did. Was he just sitting at home, obliviously watching TV, while she was going through the worst thing that had ever happened to her. Obstruction, my eye. All she was trying to do was help the police. She felt like crying, but she was not going to give any of them the satisfaction of seeing that.

"Okay, okay, back off, everybody. Mandy, Rob, I'm holding a press conference in an hour, so be at my office then. Okay," the chief shouted to the others standing there, "show's over. Everyone go on home, now. There's nothing to see here."

As he said that, Butler pulled up in the police boat that didn't have a scratch on it from Tobin's boat, thanks to Maggie. In a way it didn't seem fair she wasn't being lauded for saving all their lives instead of arrested, but Doan always knew what he was doing so he kept his own counsel on that thought.

The chief rushed Maggie into the nearest patrol car, even though they were across the street from the police station. He could have walked her across and into the building, but idiots have been known to plow right through a crowd of police officers and others in the street, barely missing some of them and he would never forgive himself if he let anything happen to Maggie. After all, he was just doing this for her own good and to hopefully cure her of her damned sleuthing.

When the officer brought Maggie into the station, he told him he'd handle it from there. "But don't you want us to process her, first, Chief?"

"I said I'd handle it, didn't I?" Doan said, glaring at the befuddled officer who was just trying to do what he was supposed to do. "Thank you, officer. Come on, let's get you upstairs, Maggie."

TEN

"Let me go," Homer shouted. "I'm going up there, through you or around you. I don't much care which it is!" He squeezed against the side railing as he tried to get around the cop who was trying to stop him.

Hearing the commotion and recognizing the voice, Butler yelled, "It's okay. Let him come up, Sherman."

Homer grinned at the young cop and went on up the stairs. The grin faded when he went through the door to Doan's office. "This is the way you locate her for us? What the hell? I heard she was under arrest."

"Oh thank God, you're here, Homer," Maggie told him, turning around in her seat. "Yes, he arrested me. I knew you'd come to help me."

"Sit down, Homer," the chief said.

"I'll stand."

"That wasn't a request. Now, if you don't want the cuffs on you, too, you'll sit down."

Homer did as he said and sat in the nearest chair next to a large palm tree that looked like it could stand some watering with more brown than green fronds. The glare stayed on his face. He did have a small smile for Maggie, who looked as scared as he'd ever seen her look.

"Now, if everyone will just calm down, I'll tell you why Maggie was arrested."

"So, it's true? You really did arrest her?"

"Of course, I arrested her. Why else would she be sitting here in cuffs?"

"But why? This is Maggie, Doan. You don't go around arresting little old ladies, especially when it's Maggie!"

"Most little old ladies don't commit serious offences, Wiley."

"What serious offense could Maggie Metronia have committed that made you cuff her like a common criminal?"

"If you'll be quiet for just five minutes of your irritating life, you'll find out. I'm only allowing you to be in here to keep you out of trouble downstairs." Looking at Maggie, he said, "Now, Ms. Metronia, I arrested you because you jumped on that boat and . . ."

"I did not jump on that boat!" she said.

"See there, she didn't do it." Homer interjected.

"I climbed in the boat like a lady," she told him, leaving Homer with his mouth open.

"Both of you be quiet. Now!" He waited for a moment and then he continued. "I arrested you because you *climbed* into that doctor's boat and obstructed our arrest of him."

"How did she . . .?"

"Shut up, Wiley!"

"Yes, how did I obstruct your arrest? You got on the boat and got him, didn't you? A boat that would have crashed if I hadn't taken the wheel!"

Homer beamed. "You took the wheel? I'm proud of . . ."

"Shut up!" the chief shouted. "Jaysus, will you two just shut up so I can do the job the city is paying me to do!" For a moment he put a hand on both sides of his head because his temples were throbbing. He reached in a drawer and pulled out an aspirin bottle, dry swallowing two of them before he did anything else.

When they were quiet, he started again. "You obstructed our arrest after you got on the boat and we couldn't get a shot at him or even at the boat, because you were a civilian and were going to drown if the boat went down when we shot at him and missed, if it sank before we could get to the man we were after." Of course they wouldn't have shot at the boat to cause the guy to drown but Maggie didn't need to know that. She said nothing. Neither did Homer.

"We had to risk our men getting shot at by climbing onto the boat to get to him rather than subduing him with a shot until we could get in the boat and take him. Sgt. Spivey and Officer Oates could have been shot by him, since they had to get so close to him – because of your being on the boat – and it was very close several times until we went aboard, and then, he sprayed Butler with fire from his automatic weapon until Oates took him from behind, and Butler and Spivey tackled him so Oates could get the gun from him." Still she said nothing. Nor did her sidekick.

"Police work is damned dangerous, Maggie. Or don't you get it, yet? It isn't fun and games or pretend sleuthing. It's serious stuff and we put our lives on the line every single time we go after someone like Tobin."

"I know that," she interjected.

"Then why did you interfere?"

"Because he was getting away and I wanted to stop him."

"And how did you propose to do that by getting on his boat?"

She hung her head. When she looked up, she said, "After I got on, I realized there was nothing I could do. And then he started the engine and I just stayed hidden."

"Well, at least you did something right."

"I saved your lives, too," she pleaded.

"Yes, you probably did when you stopped the boat from going in circles because it would have ended badly had it run into our police boat, but that does not negate the fact that you interfered with our arrest and caused us to have to put our men and then ourselves in direct line of fire from Tobin, Maggie. When, had you just stayed out of the way and gone home as I asked you to do when I saw your trike and knew you were hiding on the guy's property, none of us would have had to put ourselves in jeopardy to try to apprehend him. We would have followed police procedure in order to apprehend him without anyone getting hurt." He fell back in his seat and ran his hand through his thick black hair as he always did when he was exhausted or totally frustrated.

Thanks to the aspirin, his headache was finally starting to ease up. "You still don't get it, do you?"

"I was only trying to help the police, help you," she said in a faint voice that tore at Homer's heart, as she looked beyond Lenny at the rest of the building beyond his window. A gull appeared on a protruding edge of the building and she felt it staring at her. Her eyes were fixed on it, too, until it suddenly flew away as quickly as it had appeared.

"No, you don't get it at all. Homer, go home and call me in the morning around 9, after her bail hearing. Maybe you can take her home then."

"Lenny, please, don't do this," he pleaded. "I'll talk to her some more, get her to understand."

"Go home. Butler, take her to lock-up downstairs. We'll leave her here overnight rather than take her to the jail. It's getting late and no sense in making them do all that processing. Tell Sherman I'll take care of it when I come down and just put her in the cell. Tell Ellie to get her a blanket and pillow. Homer, I said to go home. There's nothing you can do tonight."

Maggie looked pale and frightened, but was quiet as Butler led her past Homer and down the stairs. Homer stood there not saying a word, but not leaving, either. He had no idea how to get her out of this one. He couldn't believe Doan was seriously going to lock her up in a cell. Maggie. The Maggie they all, including Doan, loved. He was really doing it. Just like the sheriff did when they were caught in the mangroves across from Alabama Jack's. She couldn't stand it then, and this will be worse, since it's her friend who ordered that she be locked up.

Doan put a hand on his shoulder. "Go home, Homer. This is for Maggie's own good."

The man turned around and stared at him. "You aren't really arresting her?"

Doan said, "Go home, Homer. Call me in the morning."

"No, you have to answer my question. Are you or are you not arresting Maggie?" He had his hands on his hips and wasn't going anywhere.

"We are detaining Ms. Metronia tonight and we'll see what happens tomorrow. I'm going now to see where my guys are on questioning the suspect, so I'm telling you to get out of my office and go home now, so I can get back to work."

Seeing that he wasn't going to get a straight answer from Doan, Homer said, "I'm going, but I'll be back first thing tomorrow, chief. You can count on that."

~ ~ ~

After he went down the stairs and Doan heard the door close, he grabbed a cup of coffee and headed down the hall to the interrogation room in which they'd taken Tobin. They'd purposefully left him in there by himself, without offering him a drink of water or allowing him his phone call.

Doan looked at Butler and nodded. Butler went into the room and closed the door. The chief took a seat in the other room and watched through the one-way window. Butler looked up at him and then told the suspect that he was turning on the video camera and to look directly at him.

Tobin did as he was told, but said nothing. There was no way he was answering any more questions tonight than he had to. His lawyer would come in and take him home. He knew his rights.

"State your full name, please, *Dr.* Tobin."

"Alexander Franklin Tobin."

"State your address, please."

105 Roosevelt Boulevard."

"Where were you at 8:00 tonight?"

"I was in my office."

"With a patient?"

"Yes, with a patient."

"What was the name of the patient?"

"Don't answer that, Alex," a voice said as a man came through the door. He handed a card to Butler. "Tom Snake, Dr. Tobin's attorney."

Butler snickered at the name. "You're not from around here, are you, Mr. Snake."

"No, I'm from Miami. I've been Alexander Tobin's attorney for many years and he called me earlier, saying he'd probably need me before the night was over and to head down. So, I started driving and when I saw the crime scene tape around his house and dock, I drove straight here."

"What was the name of the patient in your office at 8:00, Dr. Tobin?" Butler repeated as though Snake had not instructed his client.

"I told him not to answer that question, officer."

"Lieutenant," Butler said.

Snake sneered. "No difference, officer, lieutenant, cockroach, whatever."

Butler stood and his tall frame practically covered the attorney when he did. "What did you call me?"

Again, Snake sneered, and said, "I didn't call you anything, sir."

"That's better. Now, Dr. Tobin, what did you tell me on the boat was the reason you killed those women?"

"Don't answer that! How dare you try to weasel your way around a confession when I'm sitting right here?"

"Oh, maybe because your client did confess on the boat earlier," Butler said with a smile.

Doan stopped drinking the coffee. He knew what was coming next.

"And I suppose you read him his Miranda rights before you got him to confess," Snake said, with a big smile." Come on, Alex, we're done here, since they haven't charged you with anything."

"Hold on a minute, Snake," Butler said. "Alexander Franklin Tobin, you're under arrest for attempted murder of four police officers. You have the right to remain silent. Anything you say can and will be used against you in a court of law."

In the other room, Doan smiled and took another big drink of coffee.

"What? What are you trying to pull now, Butler?"

The lieutenant smiled then and said, "Guess what, Snake, your man here shot at four officers of the law, including the Key West Chief of Police and me, after we told him to put up his hands. So, you can't take him anywhere, unless the judge is foolish enough to grant him bail and I'm not seeing that in his immediate future."

Snake looked at Tobin and shrugged.

"What? You're just going to stand there and let this happen?"

"He's right, there, Tobin. I can't take you home when you committed a federal offense. Four federal offenses. In fact, I think you need to find yourself another attorney. I didn't sign on for this. I'm outta here."

"You can't just quit until I say you're through."

"Watch me." He tipped his hat and said, "Goodnight, Lieutenant. Nice meeting you." The door closed behind him, leaving the suspect sitting there with his mouth agape.

The chief walked in then and said, "Butler, take him downstairs so the guys can transport him to College Road."

"What's at College Road?"

"The county jail."

Looking at Butler, he said, "You're not gonna let them take me to jail?"

"To quote a smart attorney, watch me," Butler told him. Doan couldn't suppress his smile, as he finished his coffee.

ELEVEN

"Homer! I thought you'd never get back. Did you find her?"

"You'd better sit down," he told Carolyn. She couldn't have looked more frightened.

"No, he didn't. Oh dear God, tell me he didn't hurt Maggie. Please, Homer!"

He went over to her chair and stooped down, his hands on either arm of the chair, and said, "No, honey, he didn't hurt Maggie, but he very well could have. Didn't you see the news conference?"

"No, I haven't had the TV on. What do you mean – could have?" She was getting more frantic by the moment and he knew he had to tell her everything.

He stood then and said, "I'll be back in a minute, so just sit there and try to stay calm. I don't think the news is all bad, but I'll explain in a minute after I make some tea for both of us. You're gonna need a soothing drink and I've had enough beer for one day. It will only take a few minutes and I'll be right back." He turned back to her for a moment and said, "And I promise I'll tell you everything there is to tell about what happened tonight."

He barely heard her say, "Okay," it was such a weakly stated word.

He was back in five minutes, thanks to Maggie's electric tea kettle. "Here now, take a drink and let me know if I have enough stevia in it."

She smiled and said, "Yes, it's perfect, Homer. Thank you. Now please, sit down and tell me what's happened to Maggie and why she isn't with you."

"Maggie went directly to that fake doc's house."

"Oh no, did he see her? Did he imprison her? What happened? Please, just tell me."

"No, he didn't see her. She told the cops where he was in the house, and according to one of them standing outside having a smoke when I was leaving, he'd greased himself up with cooking oil or something and literally slipped right through their fingers. She saw him heading toward his boat, so she jumped into it and hid before he got there."

"Oh no, he found her, didn't he?" She took another sip of the almost scalding tea to keep her tears at bay.

"No, luckily, he didn't, and had she not been on the boat, it could have been a disaster for our guys, because when they slipped onto the boat, too, knowing she was there so they couldn't shoot at him after he got on the boat, he started shooting at them. Well, when he did that, it left no one at the helm, so Maggie slipped out of her hiding place at the stern and headed toward the bow to take the wheel."

"Maggie took the wheel of a moving boat? Oh my dear Lord, she's afraid of boats."

He laughed and said, "Well, she saw the boat going around in circles and getting closer to the police boat so her fear went out the window, Caro."

She didn't laugh, but said, "Was she able to stop it from doing that and save both boats?"

"She sure was and I'm really proud of her for stepping up to the plate on this one, as she saved all their lives. Had the two boats collided, there would probably have been a fiery explosion and God only knows how many of them would have lost their lives. Maybe all of them."

"She'll probably get a commendation for it from the city, Homer, as well as the KWPD. I'm proud of her, too. That was such a brave thing to do, especially when he was firing at the officers and they were probably firing back at him."

"Not too sure about that commendation, since right now she's in a holding cell at the station."

Her eyebrows went up in shock. "What! They arrested her?"

"Lenny put the cuffs on her before they got back to port. Rob and Mandy were there waiting and Rob probably got a photo of her as well as Tobin being led off in handcuffs. It'll no doubt be the front page photo."

"But why? She saved their lives!"

He took a long drink of his tea and set the cup back down. "Well, I think Lenny wanted to teach her a lesson this time, because she really put herself in danger with this trick, not to mention their having to climb into the boat without him being disabled, which put them in danger, too."

She looked puzzled, and he explained. "See, had Maggie not jumped onto the boat, they would have followed protocol and shot at him while there was a little distance between the boats. With her on it, they couldn't take the risk to try to disable him long enough to board the boat and take him into custody, while one stayed on the boat to steer it away from Tobin's boat. They might have hit her or he might have seen her and taken her hostage and who knows how that might have ended."

"Oh, now it makes sense," she told him. She took a big sip of her tea and it spilled on her top. She grabbed a tissue from the box nearby and frantically worked at it until she was satisfied it wasn't going to stain. Big tears dropped onto the top, also, but Homer let her cry it out, pretending not to notice. "There, well, I'm glad everyone is safe and he's in custody. He is in custody, right?"

"Yes, he's in the jail. And at the press conference, when Mandy asked if Maggie was being held as an accomplice, he told her no, that in some way, she was a big help to the case. She pressed it and asked why she was in handcuffs if she isn't being held for that reason. He told her it was complicated and he'd explain it all at a later time and abruptly told them that was all he had and he'd have more to say at the next press conference in a day or two. I could tell none of them liked that answer, but there was nothing more coming from him so they disassembled."

"Well, at least he didn't talk like she was a criminal, so that's encouraging," she told him.

"Yeah, Lenny told me to come back for her bond hearing tomorrow, but I have a feeling they won't turn her over to the court. I think he's going to have a long talk with her after she's been in custody overnight and put some conditions on her release." He got up from the chair and went to stand at the window. "At least, I'm hoping that's how it'll go down."

She joined him at the window and then he took her hand and they went out onto Maggie's front porch and sat, watching the larger than normal summer crowd of tourists go by the house. Some waved at them and they waved back. "I do, too, Homer. I'd hate to think she'll – that she'll have a record out of this. I can't see Lenny Doan doing that to her as much as he cares about her."

"I can't, either, but we won't know until tomorrow. Let's get out of here and drive up the road for dinner somewhere. What do you say?"

"I don't much feel like eating, but maybe a short drive and a nice meal will make us both feel better. Dear Lord, I hope you're right, that Lenny will just give her a stern talking to and put some restrictions on her for a while. I can't bear the thought of her being in the holding cell. Did he process her? Do you know?"

"No, I was there when he told Butler to tell the duty officer who started to take her to process her that he'd take care of it. The young officer who was obviously trying to do everything by the book looked exasperated, but he quickly changed his expression and thanked the lieutenant."

"Well, then, maybe things will go as you think then if he didn't even process her, yet. Did he leave when you did?"

"No, he said for me to go home so he could go to the interview room to see what's going on with the prisoner – the real one, I mean." He stood up from the porch swing and taking her hand said, "Come on, let's get out of here. Do you want a sweater for the restaurant in case we don't get a seat outside?"

She stood, also, and told him yes, and went up to her apartment to get it, swiping at tears as she went, since she was trying not to cry in front of him, anymore, even though he acted like he didn't see her. She knew better. He never missed a thing. She felt so sad for Maggie, being locked up in that cell for the whole night. She must be scared out of her wits in there, not knowing what's going to happen to her.

Homer had the Humvee running by the time Carolyn came back downstairs with a yellow sweater to coordinate with the yellow print dress she had on and walked out the front door, after setting the alarm they had installed when the last serial killer was after Maggie.

The ride up the highway was pleasant, despite all the traffic coming from the mainland to the island toward them. Since it was a nice night, and not too late, yet, they decided to go to one of their favorite spots on Key Largo instead of one nearer to home.

They lingered over their drinks after dinner on the deck, where a pleasant warm breeze was sweeping over them every few minutes. "It seems strange not having Maggie with us, doesn't it."

He looked at her and was thinking at the same time how nice it was, just the two of them, since he rarely had her to himself. He was still crazy in love with her and loved every moment of this night alone with her. "Yeah, it sure does. It's nice, though, with that nice breeze and not too many people out here on the deck now. Did you like your dinner?"

She laughed, and said, "Yellowtail? What's not to like?" The breeze played with her long blonde hair and made her look younger than she was, though Homer thought she always looked younger than her early 50s. She had a few gray strands throughout the blonde but she did nothing to cover it up, not that it detracted from her attractiveness.

He laughed, too. "You got me there." Looking down at the table, he asked, "Do you ever miss working, Caro?"

"Once in a while. Why do you ask? Do you miss playing at the pier?" She took a long sip of the tequila sunrise she'd been nursing for a while.

"Yeah, sometimes I miss all the activity, seeing all the friends I've had for years. I never made much money, but it was a nice life, you know?"

"I suppose it could be, though all that walking in circles you did most of the night sure didn't seem like an easy way to make a living to me. I don't even know how you played those pipes with all the walking. I'd just be too dizzy and breathless to play them."

He smiled. "The walking helped me to play them. I kept my momentum while walking and it wasn't like I did small circles, which could make one dizzy. If you ever noticed, I pretty much walked the whole area that was mine for the night. When you do it like that, you don't get as tired and you don't get dizzy at all. And when did you ever see a bagpiper standing still playing the pipes, except at a funeral?"

She just smiled. "Would you like another beer? I'm buying this round. Since I'm not driving, I'm going to have another sunrise before we go home."

"Sure, I'll have another, thanks." He watched as she signaled the waiter to bring them another round and then said, "You know, I feel a little guilty that we're out here enjoying this nice breeze after having our favorite dinner and our favorite drinks and Mag's – and she's sitting alone in that cell all night. I hope Ellie got her a decent dinner, anyway."

"I'm sure she did, Homer. She likes Maggie as much as everyone else does." She took a sip of the freshened tequila sunrise after the waiter took away her glass and Homer's bottle, receiving a big smile of thanks from her. "She probably sent out for a nice dinner for her and maybe even sat down and had a dinner of her own to keep her company."

"You're probably right. Can't help but worry about her, you know, since we've rarely been apart since she got that house on United."

"You knew her for a very long time before she got the house, didn't you? You're bound to feel sad, guilty and all kinds of emotions, knowing she's in a holding cell. But, remember, Homer, you said the chief told the officer he'd take care of it when he started to book her. And from that you didn't think he was going to process her at all."

"True, and yes, we've known each other since the early '80s, when I was still a kid in my mid-20s and she was around 40. You should have seen her then, Carolyn." He smiled and told her, "She had the most beautiful smile. And of course, that hourglass figure she still has, despite being in her 70s."

She smiled back at him and looked thoughtful for a few moments and he looked out toward a couple fishing boats coming in toward the shore, their lights on but low, wondering whether they caught much all day. He was a night owl and frequently went over to the bight or seaport to watch the activity with the fishing boats getting ready to go out to make the day's living. He did a lot of fishing, himself, from the boat he'd bought after Maggie won Powerball and started paying him $5000 a month.

"Homer," she said, suddenly. "When Maggie gets home, let's try again to get her to go see Dr. Troxel. Try to convince her there are no microchips in the implants. Maybe Dr. Troxel could even find an old one he had to remove from someone's mouth and slice it in two with a strong cutting instrument so she could see there's nothing inside of them except the metal they're made of – titanium or whatever it is."

He looked back at her. "Sounds like a plan. We probably can't pull it off, but we'll call Dr. Troxel to see if he'd go along with it. I know he'd love to see her get them so she could have that smile back. Although he's never really seen it since he didn't know her then, I showed him a photo of her back then and he agreed that smile should be seen."

"Oh, I didn't know you had a photo of her before she had the problem and lost the teeth. Do you have it with you?"

"I probably do." He got out his wallet and looked through it, but came up empty until he slid his finger into what looked like an empty space and there it was. "Here you go."

She took it and smiled as soon as she looked at it. "Oh my heavens, you're right. That's a gorgeous smile. Well, we just have to work on that plan as soon as we get her home and she settles in again. I know she'll probably be a bit down over the experience so we can't mention it to her right away, but sometime in the near future, we need to do it." She handed the photo back to him. "You weren't so bad, yourself," she said, grinning.

He laughed. "That was another guy in another lifetime. You about ready to head for home?"

"Yes, looks like traffic's getting heavier, already, so I think it's time." She threw several large bills on the table for the waiter, before they stood and walked to the front of the restaurant, where he paid their bill. They walked to the car, a few feet away, and were treated to the bright super moon. It seemed to light everything on the ground. She smiled at Homer as they looked back at each other. He held her door for her and she thanked him. Because she was a tall woman, her climb into the Hummer wasn't as difficult as it was for shorter women, like Maggie. She smoothed her dress after she got seated and fastened her seat belt.

When he opened the driver's door and got into his own seat, he fastened his belt before starting the car and turning on the headlights. He looked at her and smiled. "All set?"

"I am," she answered. "Thanks for a pleasant night, Homer. I think it helped to soften the blow of not having Maggie with us, but in that lonely cell."

"I hear Ellie plays a mean hand of gin rummy. Wouldn't doubt if we hear tomorrow that she stayed late to play a few hands with Mag after eating dinner with her. I could tell she was feeling bad for her before I left. And she got her a couple blankets for the bunk and a big fluffy pillow, as Lenny asked her to do. I saw her walking toward the holding cell with them. So, I think she probably went out of her way to make sure Maggie didn't feel alone tonight, at least until lights went down and she had to go to sleep."

"I expect you're right. The few times I've been around Ellie, she seemed very kind-hearted." She was quiet for a moment and then said, brightly, "I have just had the greatest idea!"

Looking at the road that was thick with traffic, coming and going, he asked, "Yeah? What's your great idea?"

"I want to stop at Walgreen's before we go home to see if they can enlarge that photo of the two of you and frame it before we leave the store. Then we can put it right at the end of the hall so Maggie will see it every time she walks into the house."

"And plant a seed in her head that maybe she'd like to have her smile back?" He grinned to himself, as he didn't dare take his eyes from the road the way some fools were passing in a dangerous no passing zone.

"Exactly." She smiled, too, thinking how nice it would be to see that smile of Maggie's every time any of them walked into the house. If that wouldn't be incentive to go see Dr. Troxel, nothing would.

TWELVE

"How large do you want it?" The clerk was holding up a chart of different sizes for them to choose. She was patient with them as they stewed over it. Because of the late hour, they were the only customers she had. She looked tired, as though she needed to go off duty soon.

"Is it almost time for you to go home?" Homer asked.

She smiled. "Is it that obvious?"

"Yes," Carolyn told her. "You look very tired."

"I admit it, I am, but I only have an hour to go until I can wrap it up for tonight."

They both smiled at her. "I think that 20x20 would be perfect," Carolyn said, looking at Homer. "What do you think?"

He grinned, not really wanting one that large of him, but this was for Maggie and it was her beautiful image they were interested in highlighting. "Sure, sounds great."

"Okay, then, have a seat and I'll have it ready in a jiffy. Oh, did you choose a frame, yet? You can look at the ones on aisle 9 or choose one here."

"I like that one in antique white, with the oval matting." Carolyn said. "It's perfect for the hallway." He nodded to the young clerk and she got it down to have ready when she had the photo enlarged.

A few minutes later, she handed it to Homer. "Is this going to work for you?" she asked both of them.

"I love it!" Carolyn looked at her friend, who agreed it did look nice, so the woman wrapped it carefully and then slid it into a large box that was made for that size.

"Thank you," they both told her and left the store after Homer paid her. Carolyn slipped her a large tip, smiling when she protested, as she walked away with him.

"I'm excited about this," Carolyn told him, as she once again fastened her seat belt for the short trip to the house.

"I agree, I think it will give Mag a lift when she sees it. You did good, Caro." He drove into the small parking lot at the side of the house, and turned off the headlights.

"I know it will. And I pray it will have the right effect upon her and like you said, be an incentive to go along with us on the implant idea."

They stood back at the entrance to the hallway and gazed at the photo. Homer was the first to break from it. "It looks great, "he admitted. "And after that long drive, I'm ready to call it a night. How about you?"

"Yes, I'm tired. Now, even if I'm still sleeping when it's almost time for you to go to the bond hearing, please yell at me to get up because I want to be there to support Maggie."

"Of course, now go get some sleep and don't worry about her. I have a good feeling about it." He smiled at her and after she returned his smile, she walked up the stairs to her third floor apartment as he turned toward his room two doors from Maggie's. He always slept in the same bedroom so he could hear if either of them needed help. He was asleep as soon as his head hit the pillow. Carolyn lay awake for a brief while thinking about their friend and benefactor, and then, she also went to sleep for the night.

The chief saw them as they walked up to the police department. They both looked anxious and he didn't blame them. He opened the door for them and they greeted each other. "Come on up to the conference room," he told them. "Maggie's already there with Butler."

They hurried up the stairs and turned toward the large conference room. Maggie's eyes widened when she saw them, but she didn't smile. She was too scared for that, thinking the worse was in store for her, with the coming bond hearing they'd talked about last night.

Both Carolyn and Homer had bright smiles for her, though, and each was thinking she'd aged ten years since yesterday. She'd always had such a youthful look about her. Perhaps it was just because she looks so scared. Or because she wasn't smiling as she always did when they greeted her after an absence of any length. Or maybe it's just plain guilt over what she'd done last night.

The chief asked them to sit on his side of the table, not beside her. He wanted to make this as isolated and uncomfortable for Maggie as possible. "Well, folks, time to get this meeting started. Carolyn, Homer, thank you for coming, but I will ask that you do not speak during the meeting. This is serious business and I want no interruptions. Do you understand?" He looked intently at both of them. They nodded that they understood and the meeting began.

"I am turning on the video recorder now, just to make you all aware of it. No objections will be noted. It is necessary to have it on." He looked at the three of them and they all nodded their assent. He turned it on. "Now, Ms. Metronia, do you understand why we're having this meeting? You may answer the question."

A pale Maggie said, in a whisper of her usual voice, "Yes, I do." Carolyn could have cried at the weakness of her reply, but she remained silent.

"Could you explain to all of us why you believe we are having the meeting?"

"I – I suppose it's because I went to the – the doctor's house and then got on his boat, after you told me to stay out of it and go home." She chewed on her lower lip.

"That's exactly why we're here. You've interfered before in our investigations, but we let it go with an admonishment, but this time you've gone too far. Do you understand this? That this time you've crossed the line?"

"Yes, I know that is why you're upset with me."

"It has nothing to do with whether I am or am not upset with you, Maggie. It has everything to do with your coming back when I told you to go home and then getting onto that man's boat, knowing he'd killed that young woman because you and Carolyn saw it with your own eyes!" His voice was raising and Maggie was shrinking down into her chair. "And to make matters worse, there was no way that we could subdue that suspect before we got onto that boat, no way we could shoot him in the arm or leg to make him vulnerable to arrest. And that was all because of you, Ms. Metronia!"

As much as she didn't want to cry, her tears started rolling down her face, which made her angry because she didn't like looking weak. "I know," she told him.

"Maggie," he said in a calmer voice this time, "why, when you have all the money in the world and could spend your time traveling with your friends here or doing any number of nice things to enjoy yourself, why do you spend so much time trying to prove you're a good investigator? You are not a licensed investigator, so please, can you tell this group – and me – why you jump into every murder investigation this department has?"

"I don't know why," she answered in that weak voice again. "I've been like this since I was a little girl and living up north where it got ice cold in winter and there wasn't much for little children to do except stay indoors, playing board games or sit around daydreaming. I mostly did the daydreaming." They all smiled at her. "I would fancy myself as an important person, like Nancy Drew or Sherlock Holmes. I just always have wanted to be an investigator."

"Then why didn't you train to be one when you were young enough to pass all the physical tests. I know you would have passed all the rest, because you're a smart lady. Why didn't you ever do that?" Butler asked her, in a kind manner, surprising Homer.

"I really don't know why. I guess I should have, then I'd be helping you instead of . . ."

"Instead of always interfering in our investigations," the chief finished for her. "Yes, the time for being a sleuth was in your younger days,

Maggie. Now it's too late and you're in serious trouble. Very serious trouble."

"I know," she answered, looking sad again. How was she ever going to get out of this mess? He was going to throw the book at her this time. He wasn't fooling around. He meant to make her pay for her actions last night.

"Maggie? Did you hear what I said?"

"You said it was too late and I was in serious trouble."

"No, after that."

"I didn't hear anything after that," she told him, puzzled.

"Well, while you were somewhere else, I said I didn't know what the judge would do this morning, that because you are a billionaire, he probably will impose a pretty hefty bond against your wealth."

"He'd do that, just because I'm not still poor?" Her eyes were almost meeting her eyebrows. She was getting scared again.

Carolyn and Homer stayed quiet as they were instructed to do, but they sure wanted to say something. Carolyn even was afraid Maggie would suffer a heart attack or stroke over all this. She was so pale for one who always had a fairly dark tan, despite knowing she shouldn't tan at all. She just didn't like sunscreen so never put any on before getting on her trike and starting her jaunt around the island. There was no trace of that suntan in her face at the moment.

"Maggie, the judge is going to come into this meeting in a few minutes, so you need to be thinking about how you're going to answer him when he asks you some of the same questions; thinking about how you're going to be able to dissuade him from imposing that large bond on you. Oh, here's Judge Lopez now."

A portly looking Spanish-speaking man was standing in the doorway, staring at Maggie so hard she wanted to dissolve into the large vinyl tiles beneath her chair. He didn't say a word, just stared at her, his look about as austere as one could look, and she was getting more scared by the moment. She wanted to ask if he was related to the mayor but didn't dare open her mouth.

Finally, he looked from her to Carolyn and Homer. "Who are these civilians, Chief?"

"They are Ms. Metronia's friends and housemates, Your Honor."

"If they say nothing, they may remain," he said, neither smiling nor frowning. He sat in the chair saved for him at the head of the table.

"Ms. Metronia, I'm going to interview you here rather than in a crowded courtroom, and I think every seat in that room is filled, because of the great interest in your case. It seems you have a lot of friends on this island. But, I want you to fully understand the ramifications of your actions in a quiet room rather than the courtroom. Bailiff, will you swear the defendant in, please."

Oh God, this is real. He's going to throw the book at her. She's finished. Her heart was racing and pounding in her ear, her hands were sweaty and those who saw her thought her face was getting paler as each moment went by. She was afraid she was going to faint right here in front of everyone and she couldn't remember fainting in her life.

After the bailiff swore her in, she turned around and went back to stand against the wall facing the table. No other officer was in the room except for the chief and lieutenant. The judge did not say anything for a few minutes, just stared at Maggie again. The bailiff who'd sworn her in indicated that she should go back and sit in the chair in front of her, which she gratefully did.

"Now, Ms. Metronia, on the charges of interfering with an investigation and obstructing the safe apprehension of a suspect, how do you plead?" At that moment, both Homer and Carolyn realized that there was no legal representation for Maggie. They looked at each other and Homer almost spoke up about it, but he didn't want to get thrown out of the conference room so he remained still, even though he didn't like it. She was entitled to have her attorney present.

Maggie must have come to that realization at the same moment, because she looked around to see if her attorney or any attorney was in the room and saw no one. "Ms. Metronia, I asked how do you plead?"

"I – I guess I plead guilty, but shouldn't my attorney be present for this, your honor?" She was chewing on her bottom lip so hard it almost bled, even though she was chewing on it with her toothless gum.

"This is an informal hearing. If we were in the courtroom, your attorney would be present," he answered with a glance at the chief.

90

As though a lightbulb went off above his head, Homer thought, he's in on it. I was right! This is no hearing at all. The chief brought him in to scare Maggie! He's not going to do anything to her.

"All right, then. Can you tell this court why you think you're guilty and exactly what you're guilty of?"

"Well sir, it seems I can't help but get involved in the Key West Police Department's investigations when there's a killer lose on our island. In this one, Chief Doan told me to stay out of it."

"And you didn't stay out of it, did you?" The judge asked it in a kind but serious manner.

"I – no sir, I didn't." She glanced at Homer and Carolyn but no smile passed between them.

"Tell me exactly how you interfered from the time you and, I guess it was you, young lady," he said to Carolyn who did not react, "witnessed the defendant stick a long needle into the neck of the young woman who was found dead near the water yesterday?"

"Well, I told my friends there that I was going into the house to rest so they believed me and stayed on the back porch. Instead of going to my room, I went out the front door, unlocked my trike and rode to where I knew the doctor lived. I hid until the police got there and then I told them where in the house he was. He'd been pacing around a room on one side of the house since I arrived. The house was almost all windows so I could easily see him."

"What happened after you told the police where he was?" The judge was sitting with his hands folded beneath his chin, looking less threatening.

"Well, sir, Chief Doan there asked me to go home and I turned around, got on my trike and rode off. But then I turned around and hid again near the dock across from his house because I saw a large boat sitting there and thought if he was going to run from the police he'd probably get on the boat rather than risk getting in his car where they could just jump in theirs and follow him."

"So, you disobeyed the chief's order to go home and hid near the boat. What happened after that?" The judge looked more intrigued than upset with Maggie.

"I was right. I saw him running out the side door so I ran ahead of him and got on the boat and hid in the stern of the boat behind a big wooden box as high as the port side gunwale. Just a few seconds later, he came running up to the boat, loosened the ropes and ran to the bow to start the boat. I thought surely they would be able to jump on it and stop him but he got it started right away and took off from the dock at a fast speed."

"What did you think you were going to accomplish by getting on his boat? Did you have a weapon on you? A knife? A gun? Anything?"

"I – no sir, I don't like guns or anything that could hurt someone, so I don't carry anything with me. And to tell you the truth, after I got on the boat and hid, it dawned on me that I'd done a foolish thing because there was nothing I could do. I just didn't want him to get away."

"Well, Ms. Metronia, I agree with you that you did a foolish thing by getting on a killer's boat. And by doing so, did you realize how badly this impeded the officers from shooting at the defendant to disable him enough that they could pull up beside his boat and get on board to apprehend him without risking their lives to do it?"

"I didn't realize it until the chief told me after he cuffed me. That was when he told me to let him take the wheel from me. See, the killer left the bow to start shooting at them and the boat had no one steering it, so it was going around in circles and getting real close to the police boat. I knew I had to do something to help them so I ran to the bow and grabbed the wheel while they were all shooting at each other. I couldn't get it to stop going in circles at first but I worked with it hard and after a few minutes I was able to steer it straight and then the chief came up to the bow and took it from me, and slapped the cuff on me at almost the same time."

"As well he should have!" The judge once again became the stern person who first walked into the room and stared at her in such an austere manner. Maggie started at his tone and turned very pale again.

"I've heard enough. I'm setting bond at two million dollars. Sir," he said, directing his attention to Homer, "are you authorized to write a check for Ms. Metronia?"

"Yes sir, I am," answered Homer in a serious tone, not wanting to make things worse if this really was the real deal.

"Do you have her checkbook on your person?"

"Yes, I picked it up from her desk this morning before we came." Maybe it isn't a pretend hearing. Maybe there was nothing for the judge to be in on, after all. Damn, Maggie, how are you going to get out of this one?

"Alright, then, bailiff take the gentleman out to pay the bond and I want the whole two million dollars, since I know Ms. Metronia's worth. Is that clear?"

"Yes, sir, it is," Homer told him after he'd gulped a couple of times from the shock of what the judge had just said. Who does that? Don't they always want just a percentage? He went out the door the bailiff was holding open.

"This hearing is closed," the judge said. "Ms. Metronia, I am releasing you on your own recognizance. And you are to be in my courtroom tomorrow for your arraignment. You may go home with your friend now. Someone from the court will call you to tell you what time to be here."

"Thank you, your honor," Maggie said, with relief that at least she could go home today. No guarantee tomorrow will be the same, she feared.

THIRTEEN

"Where are we going?" The bailiff was taking Homer to the front door, instead of to the clerk to pay the bond.

The bailiff grinned and said, "You're going outside to wait for the ladies. And you are not to say a word except it went okay when you paid the bond."

Homer exhaled deeply and said, "No, I won't say anything. Thank you."

"Hey, don't thank me. I just work here. Thank the chief and the judge. It's their thing, not mine, and I suppose they have their reasons," and she shrugged, as though she had no idea why they'd pretended to have a bond hearing in a conference room. "Have a nice day," she said, and closed the door.

Homer stood under the banyan tree on the lawn and waited for Carolyn and Maggie. He was so relieved and smiling so much he was afraid he wouldn't be able to help them pull this scam of a hearing off, if he didn't start acting serious now before they came out. He didn't have long to wait, as the chief was opening the door for them five minutes later. He looked at Homer to make sure he wasn't smiling. He wasn't. He nodded to him and went back inside.

"Oh, Homer, thank you for writing that check. I wouldn't have been able to hold the pen if they'd told me to do it. I can't believe he ordered me to pay that much, though."

"Well, everyone on the island knows you won that Powerball jackpot, Maggie. Of course, he was going to want a lot to guarantee you would stay in town to face the music."

"I agree with her, Homer. That was an awfully lot to demand of a woman Maggie's age and with her having no record, too!" Carolyn was seething and didn't care who knew it. "The nerve of the guy. Had she been able to have her lawyer present, he'd never have gotten away with it."

"Hey, it's okay. Don't let it ruin your day. I'm just thankful he let me out on my OR. He could have had the bailiff take me to the county jail, you know. So, let's just all get in the Hummer and go home. I want to fix a big breakfast and then take a long nap in my own bed." She did look very tired, they noticed, but not nearly as pale now that she was going home.

"Didn't Ellie bring you breakfast this morning?" Homer asked.

"She did, but I could only drink the coffee. The breakfast would have come right back up had I taken a bite. Let's go now, please."

"Okay, but we'll fix the breakfast and you just rest," he told her, with Carolyn concurring by shaking her head yes. When they got into the car, Carolyn, who was in the front seat with Homer, as Maggie always sat in the back because she liked the idea of having a real chauffer, even if he was her friend, looked over at him to see whether she could tell if the signing of a check was just a ruse, but he didn't look happy, so she sighed, knowing he must have given them a check and the hearing was for real.

Being in the back seat reminded Maggie of the movie she liked so much where the older lady and the chauffer become good friends as he drove her wherever she wanted to go. She said to Homer once when they were driving up the Keys to the mainland, "Just call me *Ms. Daisy.*" He looked blankly at her. He hadn't seen the movie, despite her having watched it several times when he was in the house. She just shrugged. One day he'll get it.

When they got to the house, true to his word, he started breakfast and Carolyn helped, while Maggie went in to lie down for a few minutes. She'd take the nap after breakfast, but she'd needed to lie down in her own comfortable bed. Carolyn wanted to talk about the hearing, but he told her no, he didn't want to have to think about it, anymore. She sighed again, knowing for sure it had been real if it upset him that much to talk about it.

She went in to get Maggie when they had a breakfast feast on the table and she had her eyes closed. She thought she was asleep and started to leave but then a little voice said, "Is breakfast ready?"

She smiled and said, "I thought you were asleep. And yes, it's ready."

"I did fall asleep. Let me just throw some water on my face to wake up more and I'll be right in. Thanks for doing this for me. I really needed that few minutes of rest."

Carolyn patted her on the arm and told her, "I'm sure you did, dear. I'm so sorry they had you in lockup last night. Did Ellie give you a good dinner, at least?"

"Oh sure, in fact, she got two great steak and potatoes dinners and stayed there and ate with me, and then she pulled out a deck of cards, of all things, and we played gin rummy till quite late," she said with a big smile, the first Carolyn had seen since all this started. "And here, I thought I was the only one who loved gin rummy that much."

"Homer told me that probably would happen," she said with a big smile. "He's heard rumors that she was quite the card shark. Like someone else we know. Come in when you're ready so nothing will get cold."

"Be right there."

Maggie was upbeat throughout breakfast. "Wow, these pancakes are so good, Homer. Or did you make them?" she asked, looking at Carolyn.

"No, he made the pancakes. I did the bacon and eggs," she replied, as she swallowed a piece of crispy bacon, and then added, "The fruit salad and yogurt is what you made a couple days ago."

"Well, it's all very good and I thank you both. I don't know what I'd do without my family here. I'm in a pretty scary situation right now and I'm trying to stay on top of my emotions, but sometimes it's hard, you know." A tear was ready to fall onto her cheek, and she swiped at it. That was unusual. Neither of them had ever seen Maggie cry before she was being questioned today and it unnerved them both.

"We know, Mag," they both said at once.

"Well, I have to get above being maudlin about it. It won't help my case at all to sit around writing the durned script, as they say, so I need to perk myself up. Hey, why don't we take a little trip to the Bahamas or Jamaica? That'll give us all a lift."

"Uh, Maggie," Homer said. "Have you forgotten you're out on your own recognizance and you can't leave town, much less the country?"

"Yes, you don't want to give them more reasons to send you to prison," her friend told her, though she hated to say it.

"Oh, you're both right," she said, as she threw her hand into the air. "I did forget the terms of my release. Oh well, we can at least go out for dinner tonight, can't we?"

"Let me call Lenny and ask him if you're supposed to be confined to the house," Homer told her. "Since you aren't wearing an ankle monitor, I don't think that would be the case, but we'd better check." He dialed the number, putting the phone on speaker after telling the chief he was going to do it.

"No, as long as she stays on the island, she can go anywhere she wishes, but the minute she crosses Cow Key Bridge, we'll pick her up again and this time we'll drive straight to College Road."

Maggie's eyes widened when she heard this and her breathing changed. With a smile, Carolyn squeezed her hand and she tried to smile back at her. Her smile didn't reach her frightened eyes.

"I promise she'll stay right here in town. Thanks for clarifying it, chief."

He turned back to Maggie. "Well, I'm sure you heard and understood that. And Mag, I think he means it. If you do cross Cow Key Bridge, even on your trike, I'm sure they'll pick you up again and take you straight to the county jail this time."

That made Carolyn angry again, but she remained silent since Maggie wanted to lift their moods. But how dare he say such a thing! They act like Maggie's a hardened criminal! It just isn't fair how they're treating this poor soul.

"Well, that's that, then, isn't it. Okay, we'll get dinner right here on the island and that will be fine with me. Let's go to Louie's. We haven't done that for quite a while." She looked at both of them and smiled.

Louie's Backyard was on the Atlantic and a popular spot with locals, Maggie not being an exception. She loved sitting up there and watching the ships heading for the Bahamas and other ports of call. Or just to listen to the waves crashing against the shore. And she always enjoyed all the gulls flying around and diving for food in the rushing water.

The rest of the day was spent quietly, playing cards and watching TV. Maggie was glad when evening came and they could leave the house to eat at Louie's. She got a shower and primped a little, by styling her long hair and even putting a bit of shadow on her eyelids and a touch of mascara on her lashes. She left her brows alone. She didn't want to start too much of a precedent on the island, since very few women wore even a touch of makeup, preferring to be free to be totally themselves. That was what set the women of the Keys apart from most of the women on the mainland. They loved not having to go through all that primping to make themselves presentable. Clean fresh faces were the order of the day, every day, for the majority of them.

~ ~ ~

"You look nice, Maggie. I don't think I've ever seen you with a touch of makeup on since I've known you," Homer said to her.

"Oh dear, I didn't want anyone to notice. I just wanted to look better than I've been looking since this awful business started. Give me just a minute and I'll wash it off," she told them.

Carolyn reached out and grabbed her arm. "Don't you dare remove it. It still looks natural and pretty on you. You have every right to try to perk yourself up after what you've been through."

"Carolyn's right, Mag. I only mentioned it, because you never wore it, but it does make you look bright and rested, and like nothing's different in your life. I doubt very much if other people who don't live with you will even notice it."

"He's right, dear. You've used very natural eye shadow and it just makes you look alert and nice. Until he said something, I hadn't noticed it. I just thought you looked rested. And that's all anyone else will think, too. So, leave it alone and grab your sweater in case it's chilly by the water."

"Okay, if you're sure. I don't want anyone else to notice it."

"We're sure," they both said at the same time and then looked at each other with big smiles.

"Let's go then and have ourselves a nice pleasant dinner and an equally nice pleasant night," she told them with a smile, too, although in her heart, she was as sad as she'd ever been since she lost her parents and brother. And as scared as a body could feel, visualizing spending years in prison for obstructing the police in their investigation and apprehension of that killer who claimed to be a doctor.

Homer felt sorry that he had to keep the little ruse between the chief and the judge to himself. Although Maggie was smiling, he could tell it was just a façade she was putting on for their sake. He knew she must be frightened as could be of the whole situation she thought she was in, and although he hated that she was feeling that way, maybe they were doing her a big favor by letting her think she was in a ton of trouble. Maybe it will keep her from doing any more sleuthing. He wasn't too optimistic but he could still hope.

"Wait! What's this? It wasn't here before." She was staring at the portrait in the hall of Homer and her.

They both laughed. "I thought you'd never notice it," Carolyn said, since she'd walked right past it twice with her head down and never saw it.

"When did you put it up there? And how did you find such a large picture of me? I never remembered having a portrait taken like that."

"Don't you remember having your picture taken with me? I've carried it in my wallet ever since and showed it to Carolyn coming from dinner the night of your hearing. It was she who thought of stopping at Walgreen's and having it enlarged for you. Do you like it?" He was hopeful, because if she did, it would make it easier for them to persuade her about the implants.

"I – I don't know that I like my likeness there for everyone to look at, but I have to admit, it's a nice picture of us, Homer. So, yes, I guess I do like it. Thank you, Carolyn, for suggesting it and getting it done. It was real nice of you," she answered with a smile for them both.

"I just wanted to do something to make you feel a bit better, dear," Carolyn told her. "I'm glad it made you smile."

FOURTEEN

Their dinner at Louie's was indeed a pleasant one. There were a few people who seemed surprised to see them – to see Maggie, in particular, since the last anyone knew she had been arrested and was in jail, awaiting a hearing. But everyone on the island liked her, whether they knew her personally or not, because she was one of those Key West characters who was quirky, but too nice to everyone not to admire. Those who did know her told her it was nice to see her and left it at that. That was one of the nice things about living on the island. People lived and let live. They cared, but did not have to know every little detail about their neighbors' lives unless such neighbor confided in them. And then all they wanted to do was help in any way possible.

Still anxious about her arraignment, Maggie managed to enjoy herself at Louie's. She just knew she would be bound over to jail after it concluded. But she went home after the arraignment, much to her surprise and relief. During the arraignment, her now present attorney, Roger Lopez, a distant cousin of the mayor he'd told her when asked, entered a plea of not guilty. The judge nixed a plea deal between him and the prosecutor. After they left the courthouse, she told him she didn't want a trial by jury.

"Why would you not, Maggie?"

"I just think it will all go faster if there's not six or twelve people having to come to the same decision. I'm entitled to trial by judge, aren't I?"

He shook his head, not believing this turn of events. "Of course, you are, but I strongly urge you to reconsider this. You're well thought of in this city and I think a jury trial would go well for you."

"Nope, mind's made up. It's simpler and I'll have a fair trial, either way."

"Okay, my dear, if that's what you want, I'll let the judge know. But if you change your mind between now and whenever your trial is scheduled, please let me know right away so I can tell him you want a jury trial, after all. Can you promise me you'll at least consider it?"

"Sure, I can promise that, but don't hold your breath," she told him with a smile.

He knew Maggie well, so wasn't holding out much hope for a trial by jury.

~ ~ ~

A few months passed in relative peace, but Maggie started every time any of their cells had an incoming call. But no call came from the police chief or the court, to her relief.

"Shouldn't they have scheduled Maggie's trial by now? It's been three months since she was arraigned, Homer."

"Hey, the way I figure it, no news is good news. Just relax about it. She'll have her day in court." He grinned at her and squeezed her shoulder. "Don't you agree? It really is good news that we haven't heard anything."

"I sure agree," Maggie told him, as she let her presence be known when she walked into the living room from the hallway. "Oh, I know the day will come, probably sooner rather than later, when they'll have to put it on the calendar, but I'm sure not going to inquire why they haven't. It does make me a tad nervous waiting for that other shoe to fall, though."

"Aw, don't even give it a thought," Homer said to that. "The less you dwell on it, the better each day will be. You're home, after all, not locked up."

"You're right about that," she said with a big grin.

"Up for another game?" He smiled, knowing she could rarely turn down a game of gin.

She turned toward the kitchen and said, "Come on, let's do it. You're coming, too, aren't you, Carolyn?"

"Sure, I have nothing else to do today, especially with all this rain. I sure hope this tropical storm doesn't develop further."

"The eleven o'clock advisory said it's going to weaken by Wednesday, so no worries on that score," he told her. "Just a couple more days of it and it will be past us and out to sea. It sure is a slow mover, though, so that advisory might have to be readjusted. I don't trust storms that move slow like this."

As they played, while eating the apple pie Maggie got out of the freezer and heated in the microwave, and drank loads of coffee since it was still early in the day, the rains came in squalls and small limbs were falling off the trees in the backyard. This didn't alarm them. They'd all been in the Keys too long to be surprised by what a storm of this magnitude did to the foliage in the area, even if it wasn't a hurricane. Maggie had the contractor put in hurricane proof windows before she moved into the house, as she wanted to watch the storms instead of shutter against them, knowing they were safe with the storm windows.

A hurricane did much more damage than a tropical storm, usually, but most Key Westers did not let a hurricane alarm them, either, and were known to keep an eye on the advisories and updates to board up and evacuate. Many of them took great pride in staying on the island during any hurricane. At least they did before Wilma hit the island. After the storm when everyone breathed a sigh of relief that she'd done little damage, a surge caused the Gulf of Mexico and the Atlantic Ocean to meet in the center of the island. Many, including then City Commissioner Clayton Lopez, the current mayor, lost their homes because of the waters standing five, six, seven feet inside them. It was not a good time to live in that part of Key West. Many up-islanders lost their homes, too, and debris crowded the Overseas Highway for months afterward. It took a few years before the commissioner got his money from FEMA and rebuilt his home. He wasn't alone, either. Many others in the Keys were in the same situation. Many gave up because FEMA was taking too long and they had to have decent permanent shelter again, but out of the Keys this time.

But this would be no hurricane, at least not according to the National Weather Bureau. And none of the three sitting at that kitchen table minded the heavy rains coming from Tropical Storm Peggy. It was the first time a storm had been named that and one of Maggie and Carolyn's friends from church who had the name was delighted that "Finally, after waiting 90 years, they've named a storm after me." They'd laughed with her and one of them said she hoped the storm would be as gentle as its namesake is. To that she laughingly told them in her thick Irish accent, "You just haven't seen me roar, yet," as she waved and started walking toward her home on Elizabeth, with her little dog on her heels.

"I love a rain you can hear," Maggie said. "It's like the earth is talking to us, telling us to be silent and listen to it cleaning the air and helping the grass to stay green and the trees and flowers to brighten." Her friends smiled. They loved to hear her talking like that after all she'd just gone through, and she did it often about a lot of things. She had always been quite the homespun philosopher.

As she looked out at the rain, slanted and heavy as tropical storms tend to be, her thoughts started to gather about what had recently happened in that small island city with that fake doctor serial killer and how she'd ended up being arrested for her part in it. She still thought they could have been more forgiving after she saved all their lives by taking the wheel of the doctor's boat as they were all shooting at each other in the stern. As much as she wanted to do what Homer said and not think about it, knowing she might be sentenced to do time frightened Maggie. A lot. It was so scary having the chief put those cuffs on her thin wrists and even scarier when he had the young officer lock her up in the city lockup even if it wasn't the county jail. Just knowing she was behind bars and couldn't walk out of that room was probably the most frightened she'd ever been in her seventy-three years.

"Earth to Maggie, it's your turn to make a move," Carolyn told her.

She looked at Homer when their friend didn't respond, but kept staring out at the rain. "Hey Mag, it's your move," he echoed. That got her attention.

"Oh, I'm sorry. There, I've melded," she said with a smile. Up to then, only Carolyn had melded.

"Where'd you go a while ago," he asked, nonchalantly, knowing full well where her mind had gone. Right back to the KWPD lockup.

"Oh, nowhere in particular. I was just enjoying this rain," she told him and smiled at them both. "Sorry you can't meld yet. I just love it when I get to meld before you, Homer."

"Well, not for long," he said, as he laid down his large meld after drawing a queen of spades and then threw down his discard, leaving him with no cards in his hand. He laughed at their astonished faces, as he called, "Gin."

"How do you do that? I never saw anyone who could meld and go out at the same time like you do, Homer Wiley! I swear, if I didn't know better, I'd think you had cards hidden in your lap or something," Maggie told him. She did not like to lose one bit. He laughed at her and started gathering his cards to count his score, as they counted their small number of points.

As they played, the rains beat down upon the roof of the back porch and slanted against all the windows on the south side of the house. Since the kitchen table was in front of a big bay window, it looked like it was coming right at them.

"Like I said, I love a rain you can hear," Maggie said to them again. "Soft rains are okay, especially when you're in a car and visibility isn't affected by them, but when you're sitting at home, relaxing like this, there's just nothing like a hard driving tropical rain storm that's pounding against everything in sight, as long as it doesn't destroy any homes or hurt anyone on its way through the island."

They both agreed with her. Homer reached over and with the remote turned on the TV to see if anything had changed about the storm. He shrugged and said, "Well, it looks like we have a few more days of it, so we'll be confined to the house for a while longer." He laughed, and said,

"Just long enough for me to win all the loose change either of you have hidden away."

"You mean like this?" Carolyn laid down all her cards except one and discarded with it. She added, "Gin!"

"Yay, Carolyn, that's showing him how to play gin rummy," Maggie said. "And here you thought you were the only one who could do that on the meld."

Homer just smiled. "Beginner's luck, not skill."

"Well, I'll be, look who the sore loser is now," she told him.

He yawned and said, "I think that's it for me. I feel a good nap coming on."

"Yeah, right, good excuse to keep from losing again." Carolyn laughed as he shrugged and put his cards down.

"I'm a bit sleepy, myself," Maggie told him, and started counting her cards.

"I'll be," Carolyn said again, "even with the big meld I had when I went out, you still win the game." As they both finished counting their cards and she wrote all the scores down on the pad beside her, she couldn't believe she hadn't won the game for a change.

"Hey, can I help it if I'm the champ of gin rummy? You two will just have to practice more when I'm not around," he gloated. "Maggie, looks like you came in second this time and our Carolyn with her great meld placed third."

As he walked away laughing, they just looked at each other and shrugged. "We'll get him next game, Mag, don't worry. He can't win every game forever. Or can he?" Carolyn asked with a giggle.

Once again, Homer was right, as the tropical storm fooled everyone and strengthened two days later as it changed directions and instead of staying curved to cross the Lower Keys to head for Central America, as predicted, it moved north toward the mainland as a cat two hurricane. With global warming, the past few hurricanes, regardless of their categories, were stronger and wreaked more havoc on everything in sight. Hurricane Peggy was no different. She roared through the Keys at 105 mph, pulling roofs off homes, leaving most of them on the ground completely demolished, and huge trees torn from their roots, while slinging traffic lights and billboards all over the highways, keeping the cities in Middle and Upper Keys and all the rest of South Florida busy trying to keep roads cleared. The power companies, Keys Energy and FPL, had to wait until the storm moved on from each area before they even could think of working to get traffic lights back up and power restored to those who lost it. Fortunately, there were no fatalities, but many were transported to the hospital with serious injuries. After hitting West Palm Beach, its new curve took it back out to sea toward the city of Freeport on Grand Bahama, less than ninety miles due east of Palm Beach, which was not spared its destructive force before it reached the ocean again.

Maggie's big home was spared any damage, but when she was still on the island as a tropical storm, Peggy's fury uprooted several of her young fruit trees, but she told Homer not to worry about it, they could plant more of them. But several homes in the Middle and Upper Keys had roofs blown off and their homes destroyed. As she roared through the Keys on the way to beat up on the mainland, she sounded like a train going by, with her hidden tornadoes that did most of the more destructive damage.

Of course, the Florida Keys had never heard the sound of a real train since 1935 when an unnamed hurricane was so strong that she took out Henry Flagler's passenger train and most of the railroad, causing the deaths of all on the train and the veterans working construction on Geiger's Key. The old timers in Key West who had transportation sailed their small boats up keys to see if they could help with the rescue of all those people, but were astonished to see that very few survived the destruction of the storm. They described seeing bodies lying on the banks, in trees, in the water and other places. They said it was the most horrifying scene anyone could witness and it took them a long time before they could close their eyes to sleep without seeing those bodies strewn all over the Middle Keys.

By the time that Labor Day Hurricane of 1935 roared through the Middle Keys, it was with a wind-speed of 185 mph and its death toll was 485. Its damage was up to over a hundred million dollars' worth, in the Bahamas, as well as in Florida. Several east coast states got hit badly, as well. That cat 5 hurricane was the worst in the country's history or in the history of hurricanes hitting land mass, followed by Camille and then Andrew.

The hurricane seemed to take Maggie's mind off her upcoming trial. But, despite her apparent insouciance about the whole business, she was hoping her attorney and the state attorney could reach a plea deal the judge would accept, where she could do community service instead of prison time. She kept that thought to herself. She didn't want to bring up the subject at home when they were busy cleaning up the branches and trees that had fallen and, elsewhere, helping others on the island who had damage. All of them, including her, pitched in wherever there was a need, as the locals tended to do on that small island known by tourists as the fun place to go on weekends or vacations. Most of them had no idea the other side of the island existed, so bent were they on having a good time while they were there, and why not, since they were on their weekends off or on a hard earned vacation. For many, that good time consisted entirely of starting to drink in the bars from nine or ten in the morning and continuing that Duval Crawl until late at night, day after day during their time on the island, ending up not being much fun for many of them. There were others for whom the crawl was not the sole attraction of this little island in the sun. They're the ones who went on the glass bottom boat, stood at the aquarium, watching the sea creatures, big and small, looked in wonder at the artifacts discovered by Mel Fisher and his crew in the wreckage of the ships, *Nuestra Senora de Atocha* and the *Santa Margarita*. They went to the Waterfront Playhouse and The Red Barn, enjoying the talented actors who made the plays so great. And for those lucky few who took the time to get to know a local or two, it was that benevolence, openness and acceptance by the locals as much as the beauty and laissez-faire atmosphere of the island that drew them back there and was the reason they not only visited, but eventually moved to the island.

The three of them worked night and day helping their neighbors clean up their yards and drag off articles, large and small, that didn't belong to them, like pieces of lumber, stop signs and all manner of artifacts sent from one end of the island to the other. After a few weeks

Key West looked like Key West again, with new trees replacing the stubs of those damaged or uprooted by Tropical Storm Peggy, when she was well on her way to becoming that furious hurricane further up the Keys. Life, as always, was back to normal and the storm forgotten except for what it did further north of them. Being back to normal included rescheduling what the courts had to cancel when the storm came through. One of those trials rescheduled was that of the bizarre and phony Dr. Alexander Franklin Tobin.

FIFTEEN

After all the excitement at the dock the night the doctor was arrested, the courthouse was packed with spectators, some even standing by the walls, as there were not enough seats for everyone. The judge had no objection this time and the fire chief assured him there were not too many in there, but not to allow any more to come in as it would be a fire hazard. The jury was seated. The opening statements to the jury had both been given and the judge was ready for the case to begin at 9 the following morning.

As they were packing up to go back to the office, Chief ASA Sam Thomblin's second chair, ASA Meggie Saurus asked, "Do you want me to see if the ME can be ready as soon as tomorrow, Sam?" Meggie was happy to be second chair. She admired her chief and thought he'd be a great state attorney if he ever ran for the office when their boss decided to step down. She was a latecomer in the state attorney's office. She had been a nurse in a big city hospital in Missouri while her four children were young. Her husband was a well-liked pediatrician in the same hospital. They'd planned to retire when they were both in their early fifties and see more of the world in which they lived. Fate stepped in when they were both forty-five, just a few years from their goal. Jackie, her husband, was hit by a speeding car while he was jogging one morning. He never regained consciousness before he died, leaving her a devastated middle-aged widow with four children in high school.

Unfortunately the driver of the car got off with a technicality and Meggie was beyond angry. Just because he had low blood sugar at one time, his attorney used that as an excuse for him to be speeding that morning. He claimed he was hurrying to the ER because he felt like his blood sugar was very low and he didn't want to pass out at the wheel and hurt someone. Well, he hurt someone, anyway. He hurt her beloved husband and killed him, just four years before they were to retire from nursing and medicine. Meggie Saurus decided then and there that she was not going to stand by and see others hurt by people like him who had no regard for the rights and lives of others. She resigned from her position in the hospital and left nursing forever. With the insurance money from her late husband, she paid off the mortgage on the house, saved enough for all the children to go to college and enrolled in law school. After she passed the bar, she moved with her youngest child, who was in her senior year of high school but ready for a new adventure with her mom, to the end of the road, Key West. She applied for and got a job as an assistant state attorney and four years later, she was still there because she loved it so much and had no desire to go into private practice.

"Yes, give her a call and see if she's ready and I'll call her first thing, if we're that far along by tomorrow," Sam told her with a smile. He was happy she was his second chair. Now in her middle fifties, she still looked young. She had the kind of face that made her look like a teenager well into her thirties and she was aging well. She was still an attractive woman with a nice friendly smile and long dark blonde wavy hair with long bangs she swept to the side. Like most Keys women, she wore no makeup and didn't need it. Meggie was the best assistant state attorney Sam had working under him. She excelled in prepping the witnesses to the process and always was totally prepared with whatever material was needed to make their case. Perhaps because she wasn't young, anymore, and had been a supervisory nurse most of her adult life until she went to law school, she paid more attention to every detail, big and small. She was quick to offer suggestions to Sam if she saw the need. He never minded, because he knew everything she did contributed to their having a more solid case than if she weren't working on it with him. She kept him on his toes and he appreciated it. He even had her give the opening statement in this case and thought she did an exemplary job on it.

~ ~ ~

"All rise. The Honorable Judge Clinton Redding presiding." The judge sat quickly and motioned for everyone else to sit.

"Mr. Thomblin, are you ready to present your case?"

"Yes, your honor. I am. The state calls Maggie Metronia."

The door opened and an officer directed Maggie to the dais. She walked up, and as directed by the bailiff, stated her name and took the oath from him. He then directed her to sit in the witness chair. She was so small, the chair swallowed her. He directed her to sit closer to the microphone and she did.

"Good afternoon, Ms. Metronia."

"Good afternoon, sir."

"Would you prefer to be called Maggie?" He smiled and she relaxed.

"Yes, please, if you don't mind."

"Okay, Ms. Maggie, can you tell the court where you were and whom you were with on the night of May 15, 2001, around 8:00?"

"Sure, I was with Carolyn Cramer and we were outside a doctor's office."

"What is your relationship to Ms. Cramer, if I might ask?"

"Yes, sir, of course. We're close friends and she lives on the third floor of my home on United."

"Will you tell the court the name of the doctor you were going to visit?"

"Yes, his name is Dr. Tobin, but we weren't going to visit him." Tobin did not look too surprised at this revelation from her. He remembered her coming in that time on the ruse about seeking a dentist who did implant surgery.

"You weren't knocking at Dr. Tobin's door in order to keep a late appointment?"

"No, sir, we didn't knock on the door at all." She sighed deeply and looked down for a moment at the royal blue carpeting that covered the courtroom floor, and then she looked back at the prosecutor.

"Will you tell the court why you were there and what you were doing?"

With a big sigh, she answered, "Well, I had my doubts that Dr. Tobin was a real doctor and I – I asked Ms. Cramer to go with me to – well, to sort of spy on him to see if we could figure out what he does for his patients, since the name on the building just says Dr. Tobin."

"How were you – as you said – spying on the doctor?"

"We saw there was a light on and knew he was in there, so we went into the alley and were standing there by a window watching him."

"Was he alone at the time?"

"No sir, he had a young woman seated across from him."

"Was this young woman seated on an examination table?"

"Harrumph!" Low snickers spread across the courtroom from those who knew Maggie or knew of her. It was a typical Bone Island Maggie response.

"Objection!"

"Ms. Maggie, please confine your comments to the answers to Mr. Thomblin's questions."

"Yes, your honor, I'm sorry." She looked confused for a moment.

"You may answer the question now."

"Oh, sure, thank you. No, there was no examination table in the building."

"How could you tell that? Could you see into all the exam rooms?"

"What exam rooms? There were no exam rooms or even an office. The doctor just sat on a chair and the patient sat right in front of him in this big room that looked like a gymnasium."

"What was the doctor doing for or to the patient, Ms. Maggie?"

"He was just talking to her."

"So, the entire time you and your friend, Ms. Cramer, were at the window until you left, that's all he was doing? Talking to her?"

"Oh no, after a few minutes he stood and went sort of to the side of her. He started rubbing her neck and . . ."

116

"Excuse me for a moment. Let me make sure I have this correctly. He was no longer sitting in the chair across from her, right?"

"Yes, that's right."

"Were you close enough that you could hear the conversation they were having?"

"Yes, but we couldn't hear it plainly until he stood beside her chair."

"Ms. Maggie, please tell the court what you heard Dr. Tobin and the patient saying and what he was doing at the time."

Maggie swallowed hard and then spoke, "As he was rubbing her neck, he asked if it ever bothered her in that spot. She started to say no, because we heard the 'n' sound, but then he took out a large fat syringe from his pocket and plunged the long needle into her neck right here in that indentation at the base of her skull." She turned her back to the ASA and pointed to the base of her skull.

"Did she act like she was expecting him to do that?"

"Objection. Your Honor, how would this witness know if she expected it?"

"Overruled," Redding told him. "Please answer the question, Ms. Maggie."

"No, she looked startled and asked him, 'What did y . . .' but she never got the 'you' out before she looked like she'd passed out."

"Passed out? Tell the court why you believe she passed out."

"Well, like I said, the only two words she got out were 'what' and 'did', and made the 'y' sound, and then her eyes closed and she slumped sort of to one side and didn't say anything else."

"What did Dr. Tobin do when this happened? Did he try to revive her?"

"Revive her? Ha!" Muffled laughter was heard and the gavel came down again. Tobin even grinned.

"Objection!"

"Sustained. Ms. Maggie, just answer the question, please, without extraneous comment," the judge admonished.

"Yes, your honor, I'm sorry. No, he sure didn't try to revive her."

"Well, what did he do if he didn't try to revive her?"

"He – he said, 'Bye bye, Ms. Kincaid,' and with one finger on her back, he shoved her to the floor."

There was a collective audible gasp from the spectators and the victim's mother started sobbing again. Thomblin waited a few seconds before he continued when she wasn't crying aloud. The judge, as before, said nothing.

"Are you sure you heard and saw what happened correctly?"

"Oh yes, there was no question about it. That's what he did and said."

"Ms. Maggie, do you see Dr. Tobin in this courtroom?"

"Yes sir, he's right there sitting between Mr. Slade and that pretty lady in the red suit," she answered clearly, causing the assistant public defender, Sally Patrick, to smile. She'd just turned 70, had snow white hair and her share of wrinkles. No one had called her pretty in quite a while.

"What did you and Ms. Cramer do when you saw this happen?"

"We stepped back and ran from the window, because we didn't know if he saw us or heard us, and we didn't want to be next."

"Objection!" Cyrus Burns, Tobin's new attorney, said.

"Overruled. Please continue, Mr. Thomblin."

"Where did you run to when you left the window? Did you hide in the alley?"

"No, sir, we just ran back down Truman until we got to United and then we ran into the street when we saw a police car coming."

"You ran into the street?" Thomblin smiled at her. "Wasn't that taking a risk the car would hit you?"

"We didn't give that a thought. We just wanted to get to safety until we reached home."

"Do you drive, Ms. Maggie?"

"Not anymore, sir, I took my life in my hands too many times on that highway, so I'm driven everywhere."

"Oh, so Ms. Cramer drove the two of you to the doctor's office?"

"No sir, we just took a walk up to the office."

"That's a distance from United Street, isn't it?"

"We're used to walking all over the island, so it didn't seem very far – well, not until we saw what we saw in that building and then it seemed we'd never make it back to United."

"What did the police officer do when he saw you?"

"He slammed on his brakes – it was Sergeant Spivey in the car and he – he knows us." She grinned sheepishly. "He yelled at us, asking something like 'do you have a death wish?'"

"Please tell the court what happened then."

"We begged him to let us in the patrol car, which he did after we told him we'd just seen a young woman murdered."

"Objection! This witness did not say she examined the patient to see if she was breathing."

"Overruled."

Burns frowned, but didn't argue with Redding. He sat back down and stretched his neck a couple times.

"Did Sergeant Spivey let you in the patrol car then?"

"Yes, he did, and he was going to take us home, but we asked him if he could check on the young woman first, in case what he gave her just knocked her out instead of killed her."

"And he did that – with the two of you in the patrol car?"

"He started to, I think, but then we saw Homer drive up and..."

"Before you finish that statement, will you please tell the court who Homer is?"

"Homer is our friend and my chauffer, Homer Wiley. He lives on Sugarloaf but when he's in town, he stays at my house. We're sort of a little family," she said, smiling at the jury with her mouth open, showing she had no upper teeth. Most in the jury smiled back at her.

"I see." He smiled at her, also, and asked, "What happened then?"

"Well, we told Spivey, er, Sergeant Spivey, to let us out and we'd ride home with Homer."

"And did he? Let you out of the patrol car?"

"Yes, sir, he let us out and told us to go straight home. He didn't have to say that twice, since we were scared out of our wits and couldn't wait to get home."

"Thank you, Ms. Maggie. That's all I have to ask you."

"Mr. Burns? Cross?"

"Yes, your honor." He walked to the dais slowly and without his usual swagger. He stood there a moment and glared at Maggie.

She wanted to yell at him to ask his questions if that was what he intended, but she didn't want the judge to speak harshly to her this time, so she just stared back at him.

"Ms. Metronia," he started, deliberately emphasizing Metronia, "is Metronia your real name?"

"Yes sir, it is." She thought this a puzzling question but did not say that to him.

"It sounds so much like the street name Petronia in Solares Hill and Bahama Village that I thought you made it up," he said with a strange smile. "Are you sure you didn't – make it up, that is?"

"No sir, I wouldn't do that. It was my parents' name."

"Thank you. Now, let me ask you this, do you wear glasses?"

"No sir, I don't need to, I'm 20/20 near and far."

"Please, just answer yes or no. Do you wear hearing aids?"

"No sir, I hear just fine."

"You don't follow instructions very well, though, do you?"

"Objection! Badgering."

"Sustained," Redding said. "Please continue and move on, Mr. Burns."

"Yes, your honor. Ms. Metronia, you enjoy sleuthing, don't you."

"Objection! Relevance?"

"Sustained. Mr. Burns," the exasperated judge said. "Rephrase your question."

"Yes, your honor. Is this the first time you've – as you told Mr. Thomblin – spied on someone?"

"Well, probably not." Snickers could be heard again throughout the courtroom. Instead of bringing down the gavel again, Judge Redding put his hand over his mouth with his thumb under his chin. He, too, was aware of the notoriety of Maggie Metronia and her spying escapades. It was difficult not to smile, but he hid it from everyone else.

"Haven't you and your friend Homer Wiley been in jail for doing this kind of thing across from Card Sound Road in the mangroves?"

"Objection! Relevance?"

"Overruled. You may answer the question, Ms. Maggie," Redding said with a smile this time.

"Yes, your honor. Well, yes, they held us but . . ."

"No further questions," Burns said, and walked back to his seat.

"Rebuttal, Mr. Thomblin?"

"Yes, your honor."

He rose from his seat and looked at Maggie. "Ms. Maggie, how long did you and Mr. Wiley stay in jail?"

"Just overnight, sir."

"Why were you released after only one night?"

"The murderers struck again," she answered.

"While you were incarcerated?"

"Yes, sir."

"Thank you. That's all I have for this witness, your Honor." He sat down again, the judge told Maggie she could go and the bailiff helped her down from the dais.

"Your next witness, Mr. Thomblin."

"I call Carolyn Cramer to the stand," he said.

After Carolyn walked into the courtroom, had reached the dais, taken the oath and sat down, Thomblin started asking her about the night of May 15, 2021, around 8. Her answer was the same as that of Maggie's.

"I was looking into a window at a doctor's office."

"Why were you looking into the window?"

She hesitated, and hung her head for a moment, then she looked up and said, "I was spying on the doctor."

"Were you alone?"

"No sir, I was with Maggie. Maggie Metronia."

"What is your relationship to Ms. Maggie?"

"She's my dearest friend and we share her house."

"Will you tell the court what happened when you were spying on the doctor through the window?"

Carolyn explained everything exactly as Maggie had, pointed to Tobin when asked if he were in the courtroom, and Thomblin told her, "Thank you, Ms. Cramer. That will be all."

"Mr. Burns, do you want to cross?" Redding looked at his watch. "Bear in mind, we're getting near the lunch hour."

"Yes, your honor, I just have a couple of questions. Ms. Cramer, do you wear glasses?"

"No sir, I've never had to wear glasses."

"Is that because your vision is so good or because you don't get checkups?"

"Oh, I get checkups every year, but my vision is always 20/20 for reading and distance.

"What about hearing aids? Do you need them?"

"No sir, my hearing has always been great. I see my ENT every year, too," she added, with a smile.

"No further questions," he said, stomping back to his seat.

"Thank you, Ms. Cramer, you may step down," Redding told her. "We'll break for lunch and be back at precisely one pm.

"All rise," said the bailiff.

SIXTEEN

After the lunch hour, Judge Redding asked if Thomblin had any more witnesses to present. He answered, "Yes, your Honor, I do. I call Sergeant Spivey to the stand."

After Spivey had gone through the swearing-in process and was seated, Thomblin asked him, "Sergeant Spivey, where were you around 8 pm on the night of May 15, 2021?"

"I was in my patrol car driving west on United."

"Did you see anyone on the street at that hour?"

"Yes, besides a handful of tourists, I saw two women running into the street."

"Were these women near your patrol car, sir?"

He smiled and said, "Yes, they ran right in front of it."

"Did you know who these women were?"

"Oh yes, I've known them for a few years now."

"Will you tell the court their names and how you know them, please?"

"Sure. They were Maggie Metronia and Carolyn Cramer. I knew them because they've been in trouble with the department a few times."

"Trouble? What do you mean by trouble? Have they broken the law a few times?"

"No, not actually broken the law. I would say they sort of interfered with the department's investigations a few times and had to be admonished for their actions."

"I take it these actions were taking it upon themselves to try to help you solve some cases?"

The sergeant laughed, and said, "You could call it that, yes."

"But they've never actually broken the law, though, right?"

"That's right."

"Let's get back to the night in question when you said they ran into the street in front of your patrol car. Why would they do such a thing that could have gotten them hurt or worse had your car hit them?"

"Well, they said they needed to get into the car because they just saw someone murdered and . . ."

"Objection!"

"Overruled. You may continue, Sergeant Spivey."

"They said they were afraid the man who did the act might have seen them and might be coming after them or words to that effect."

"So, did you let them into your patrol car?"

"Yes, they seemed quite frightened and I knew enough to take them at their word."

"Where did you take them after they got into the car?"

"I was going to take them home to the house belonging to Maggie at the corner of Duval and United, when they saw their friend Homer Wiley coming down the street toward the house and asked me to let them out so they could ride home with Homer while I checked out the doctor's office to see if the young woman might still be alive."

"And after you let them out of the car, what did you do then?"

"I turned around and went back to Truman to the doctor's office."

"What doctor was that, Sergeant?"

"Dr. Alexander Tobin."

"Do you see Dr. Tobin in the courtroom?"

"Yes, that's him sitting between Ms. Patrick and Mr. Burns." Tobin's lips curled in a sneer, but the officer ignored him.

"What did you find when you went to Dr. Tobin's office?"

"I found nothing, except Dr. Tobin who was there in the process of turning out the lights."

"What did you do then?"

"I told him to leave on the lights and asked if I could search the building. He gave his consent so I searched for the woman the ladies told me about."

"Did you examine the young woman, Ms. Kincaid?"

"No sir."

"Why not?"

"She wasn't there. There was no one there except Dr. Tobin." Tobin and Burns looked smug and Patrick smiled at them.

"Did you look in the front of the office, in the waiting area?"

"Sir, I searched every inch of the building, under the receptionist desk, under the chairs, everywhere, but found no sign of anyone else."

"Did you ask to search the doctor's car?"

"Yes, I did."

"And did he allow such a search?"

"Yes, he even opened the trunk for me but there was nothing to be found. The car was as clean as the office."

"So, what did you conclude as a result of your search?"

"I concluded that the women were telling the truth, but that he'd done something with the body before I got there."

"Objection!"

"Overruled."

"How did you reach this conclusion, Sergeant, when you saw no evidence she was there?"

"When I was by his car, I felt the hood and it was hot like it had just been driven."

"Why did you do this?"

"If it had been driven, it could mean that he somehow had known the women were at the window, so he'd hurried and disposed of the body somewhere else and then rushed back to the office, knowing at some point we'd come by to talk with him."

"Objection, conjecture!"

"Overruled."

"How much time do you think had elapsed since you first saw the women until you got to the doctor's office?"

"I'd just checked my car clock right before I saw them and it said 8:05. When I reached Truman and the doctor's office, after speaking with the ladies and then letting them out of the car into Homer's Humvee, it was 8:30."

"So, twenty-five minutes had gone by when you finally reached the doctor's office on Truman?"

"That's correct, sir."

"Let me ask you, Sergeant, did you ever see Ms. Kincaid that night?"

"Yes, sir."

"Where did you see her and in what condition was she?"

"I saw her lying by the water on Smather's Beach. I'm sorry to say she was deceased."

Once again, there was audible crying by Mrs. Kincaid, the mother of the dead woman. Thomblin remained silent for the few moments it took her to get herself under control and stop sobbing aloud. Then, he said, "Did you see signs of a struggle on Ms. Kincaid's body?"

"No sir, just like the other young women . . ." ASA Meggie Saurus glanced at the jury at that moment and all of them looked shocked to hear there might have been other young women the phony doctor had killed. Up until that moment, the KWPD had kept quiet about the other young women seemingly washed up on shore, dead. All four of them were tourists who'd come alone to the island so there was no one there looking for them.

"Objection, this trial is about one young woman, not others."

"Sustained. Sergeant, please rephrase your answer."

"Yes, your honor. No sir, Ms. Kincaid was fully dressed and looked peaceful, like she was sleeping, until the officer who found her checked for a heartbeat and found none."

"And what was the name of that officer who found the deceased?"

"That was Officer Thon Yamahana, sir." The stenographer looked up at the judge and he asked Spivey to spell the other officer's name, which he did.

"And what did Officer Yamahana do after he ascertained Ms. Kincaid was not breathing?"

"He called me and I called crime scene and the ME, while I was driving to the scene."

"Thank you, Sergeant Spivey, I have no further questions."

"Mr. Burns?"

"No questions, your Honor, but I reserve the right to question this witness at a later time."

"You are still under oath, Sergeant, but you may be excused for now."

"Yes, sir," Spivey told him.

After the sergeant walked from the dais, the judge said, "I believe that will be all for today, Mr. Thomblin. Do you have other witnesses?" Thomblin indicated that he did. "Well, then, you may conclude your questioning in the morning. This court is adjourned until 9 am tomorrow morning." The gavel came down and the courtroom stood while Redding left the room and then the buzzing started among the spectators and the press, as the lawyers packed up and the prisoner was taken back to his cell in the county jail on College Road between Key West and Stock Island.

SEVENTEEN

When court reconvened at 9 am, Thomblin called Medical Examiner Amy Smerda. M.D. to the stand, and after the swearing-in process, he said, "Good morning, Dr. Smerda, thank you for taking time from your busy schedule to appear this morning."

"My pleasure, Mr. Thomblin."

"Now, Dr. Smerda, did you receive a body in the morgue at some point during the night of May 15, 2021?"

"Yes, sir, we received just one that evening, at 10:05."

"And was that body male or female?"

"The body was female."

"Did she have any identification on her?"

"Yes, sir, she had a small cross-body purse."

"And what was her name, doctor?"

"The name in her wallet and on all her credit cards was Lily Kincaid."

"Was she a local or tourist?"

"She had a local address."

"Was there anything in her wallet or purse that told you if she was employed locally?"

"Yes, sir, it indicated she was a librarian at the Monroe County Library on Elizabeth and Eaton Streets."

"Thank you, Dr. Smerda. Did you begin the autopsy on Ms. Kincaid right away?"

"No sir, I waited until after the next of kin were located and had come to the morgue to verify her identity."

"Who was or were the next of kin and were they local, also?"

"Her parents, John and Rose Kincaid, who also live here in Key West."

"Thank you. And after the parents left, did you then begin the post?"

"Yes, sir, it was still relatively early and there was no reason to wait. I had no more bodies that had not already been autopsied."

"Was there another reason you did not wait until morning to do the post on Ms. Kincaid?"

"Yes, sir, the chief wanted a COD that night."

"The chief?"

"Yes, Chief Lenny Doan, of the Key West Police Department."

"Will you please tell the court what you mean by a COD?"

"A COD is cause of death."

"And did you determine the cause of death that night?"

"I determined the method of death, but not the cause of death," she replied.

"I don't understand. Will you please explain what you mean by that statement?"

"Certainly. I determined that she had been injected by a long needle at the base of her skull into the brain through the spinal cord."

"Why did you determine it was a long needle?"

"Because it had reached the brain."

"I understand. Can you show the court where this was?"

She turned around and pointed to the small indentation at the base of her own skull where the brain begins, just as Maggie Metronia had done when he was questioning her.

"If you know she was injected, why couldn't you determine the COD at that time?"

"I had to wait for the toxicology screen to come back before I could say what the substance was in the needle by which she was injected."

"And did the tox screen show this to you?"

"Yes, it did."

"And what was this substance?"

"It was ethylene glycol, Mr. Thomblin."

"What is that in laymen's terms, doctor?"

"When mixed with distilled water, ethylene glycol becomes antifreeze."

The victim's mother screamed, and then looked as though she might faint. Thomblin looked at the judge and he asked the bailiff to take her a drink of water. After a few moments, she was still visibly upset, but was quiet and her color had returned. The bailiff asked her quietly if she wanted to leave the room and she declined to leave, saying she needed to hear every word. She smiled at her and went back to her post at the front of the courtroom.

"You may continue, Mr. Thomblin."

"Thank you. How much ethylene glycol was in the victim's system?"

"There was 100 milliliters in this victim's blood stream."

"Would you consider that a lot, doctor, and was it enough to cause death?"

"Oh yes. Just 90 milliliters would be lethal to someone who weighed 135-140 pounds." The victim's parents both gasped loudly.

"And how much did Ms. Kincaid weigh?"

"She weighed 105 pounds."

"How long would it have taken 100 ml of ethylene glycol to kill Ms. Kincaid?"

"Inserted into the base of the brain the way it was, it would have meant her death was instantaneous, within two or three seconds. She would not have had time to suffer from the injection," she added, for the sake of the parents.

"Thank you, Dr. Smerda. That is all I have for you."

"Mr. Burns?"

"Yes, your honor, I have a few questions. Dr. Smerda. What are your qualifications to give this type of testimony?" This made Thomblin smile, because he knew her background.

"Of course. I attended Harvard Medical School, interned at Massachusetts General Hospital for one year and also had five years of residency in forensic medicine and pathology there. After that I was a fellow in forensic medicine and pathology, working directly under the medical examiner of Cuyahoga County in Cleveland, Ohio for two years before I was offered and accepted the position of chief medical examiner for Boston, Massachusetts. I remained there for twenty-one years before coming to accept the position I'm in now as chief medical examiner for Monroe County. I've been here for eleven years, Mr. Burns."

"Thank you, Dr. Smerda. I have no further questions of this witness, your honor."

"You may step down, Dr. Smerda," the judge said. After she left the courtroom, he asked Thomblin if he had any more witnesses and he said he did not, that the state rests. "This court is adjourned until 9 Monday morning."

Before they left the courtroom, Thomblin spoke with the Kincaids, offering his apologies for what they'd just endured. "I know that was terribly difficult for you to hear, but the jury needed to hear it."

"Mr. Thomblin," Mr. Kincaid said, "we needed to hear it, too. If it helps to put that animal away for the rest of his life, any grief over what we hear in this courtroom will be worth it." His wife nodded her head, but could not speak for crying. He put his arms around her and held her close to his chest while she continued to sob. Thomblin briefly put his hand on her back and shook hands with Mr. Kincaid before he turned to leave the courtroom, saying no more, but nodding to his second chair, ASA Meggie Saurus, who then quietly escorted the couple out of the courtroom by a side exit so they wouldn't have to endure questions by the press and TV reporters. Sam Thomblin would handle them.

EIGHTEEN

Cyrus Burns, the chief assistant public defender, unlike the chief assistant state attorney who was dressed for the tropical weather, was dressed to the nines in a solid black suit with bright red accessories – tie, handkerchief and socks. His black dress shoes were impeccable in their shine. Burns was a 56 year old portly bachelor who had been the chief assistant public defender for the past ten years, so chosen by his boss five years after he became an assistant public defender. He had no desire to go into private practice where he knew he'd certainly make more money or to try to be elected as *the* public defender. His boss, Joe Sexauer, could keep that job. Too political for him. And although many assistant public defenders who wanted to be chief protested Burns' longevity in the position, Sexauer paid them no heed. He knew a good thing when he saw it and he knew that Burns was the best trial lawyer he'd ever had, even better than he was, although no one ever heard him admit to that.

"You may call your first witness, Mr. Burns," the Honorable Judge Clinton Redding told him. Redding had been on the bench for 30 years in Key West and was happily preparing to announce his retirement next week if the trial was over by then. The white haired African American widower, who did not like to think of himself as African American because he told people he was born in America and even though he might have been descended from African ancestors, he was an American. He'd tell them people born in America who were descended from ancestors in France, for instance, were not called French American. It was a big issue with him and he'd correct anyone who happened to refer to him as African American. Redding was a handsome slender man of 75 who had café au lait skin tone. His father's skin was a bit darker than his. He was also born in America, and his mother emigrated from Ireland. They were both in their late 90s and still going strong. He hoped to convince them to travel the world with him after he retired. This was going to be his last case, though no one else knew it, yet.

"I call Dr. Alexander Franklin Tobin to the stand," Burns said in a loud voice, though Tobin was sitting right there beside him. Of course, loud murmuring was heard throughout the courtroom. Redding pounced on it with his gavel and everyone stilled. No one wanted to be singled out or worse, thrown out of the courtroom during this sensational trial and especially when the accused was taking the stand. Redding never hesitated to do so if someone was recalcitrant about obeying his rules.

Tobin was impeccably dressed, also, but not in a suit. He wore a white dress shirt that was made to be worn outside his trousers, which were light beige with creases down the front that could have cut a piece of paper. He wore a pale yellow tie and handkerchief. On his feet were polished brown loafers without socks. His hair was slicked down and not a hair blew out of place when he stood and walked under the AC vent on his way to the witness box. He had a deep tan, since most of his time was spent out by or in his pool. When he was sworn in, Burns started questioning him.

"Please state your name again."

"Dr. Alexander Franklin Tobin," he replied in a quiet voice.

"I'll need you to sit closer to the mic so your voice will be heard throughout the courtroom, Dr. Tobin."

"Oh, sorry," he said as he scooted a bit closer to the microphone.

"Thank you. Dr. Tobin, where were you on the night of May 15, 2021?"

Tobin gave a small laugh and said, "I don't keep dates in my head, Mr. Burns. I'm sorry."

"Do you have your appointments on your phone calendar?"

"Yes, I do," was his answer, but he didn't get out his phone.

"Check that date in your calendar now." It was not a request and Tobin quickly got out his phone.

"Oh, I had an appointment that night," he told him, as though no one had testified to that appointment on the 15th of May.

"What was the time of your appointment?"

"Let's see. It started at 8:00 and ended around 8:15."

"Since it was that late, I assume it was not with a patient."

"Oh, to the contrary, it was with a patient, Mr. Burns. I accommodate my patients, not the other way around."

"That's generous and kind of you, Dr. Tobin," the attorney told him, to disgruntled murmurs from the crowd, causing the gavel to come down again, harder this time. When the room was silent again, Burns continued. "Are you at liberty to give us the name of this patient, doctor?"

"Yes, since the patient is deceased, confidentiality no longer holds." There was an audible sob from the mother of the young woman as he said she was deceased. "Her name is – sorry, was Lily Kincaid."

Ms. Kincaid's father's hands fisted and his jaw muscles tensed, but he said or did nothing to get himself removed from the courtroom. His wife was openly sobbing now, but it was quiet and the judge said nothing.

"Was Ms. Kincaid very ill when you saw her that night?"

"Oh no, to the contrary, she was in the best of health."

"That seems strange if she asked to see a doctor, especially so late."

"No, my patients sometimes just want to talk to me if they're having a problem or to get affirmation that they're doing the right thing in their lives at the time."

"Oh, I see, and was Ms. Kincaid having a problem she wanted to talk about?"

"Yes, she was, but I don't feel comfortable telling the court what it was."

"That's not necessary. I wasn't going to ask you the nature of the problem. Did she seem to believe she'd resolved whatever it was before she left that night?"

"Yes, she seemed relaxed after we talked for a while."

"What time did you say she left your office, Dr. Tobin?"

"It was around 8:15, I believe."

"Thank you, doctor; that will be all."

Tobin started to get out of the witness chair, when the judge asked him to remain seated. "Do you want to cross, Mr. Thomblin?"

"Yes, if it please the court, I would," Sam Thomblin told him, after handing both Burns and the judge a sheet of paper. The chief assistant state attorney was twenty years younger than the chief assistant public defender, and at least six inches taller, at six feet, five inches. He was a handsome lightly tanned young man of 36, slender but he could not be called skinny, as he worked out every morning before he left home and every evening before he returned. As a result, he was well-endowed with noticeably toned but not bulging muscles. Unlike Cyrus Burns, he wore a pale blue shirt tucked into dark gray slacks, a dark blue tie and dark blue socks, with dark gray shined leather loafers. His eyes were large but not bulgy, heavy lidded and they were such a pale blue they almost looked colorless. Women found him handsome, but he was married to another assistant state attorney who handled sex crime investigation, Lola Bridger-Thomblin, a beautiful native Hawaiian, as sweet as she was beautiful, but tough in the court room, and he was quite proud of her. They'd been married for four years, but had no children, purposefully waiting until they left the State Attorney's Office and had their own practice for a couple of years. Then they would consider whether they wanted to become parents at that time.

Thomblin walked to stand in front of the witness box, careful not to get closer than allowed. He stared, unblinking, at the witness for what seemed to be fifteen minutes, but in reality was only ten seconds. Tobin reached up and ran his finger beneath his collar. Beads of sweat popped out of his forehead. "Will you please state your name again?"

"I've already said it twice."

"Answer the question, please," the judge admonished.

"Yes, your honor. My name is Dr. Alexander Franklin Tobin."

"But you aren't really a doctor, are you?"

"Of course, I'm a doctor. You don't put Dr. before your name if you aren't one."

"May I see the license in your wallet, please?"

"My driver's license? Sure," and he started to take it out.

"No, your M.D. license. I'm sure you must carry it with you," he added, not having any idea if physicians had small versions of their license to carry in their wallet.

"What? Why would I do that? I do carry my business cards, though."

"May I see a business card?"

"Here you go," Tobin said as he handed it over to the imposing-looking attorney.

Thomblin looked it over slowly and then thanked him and gave it back. Once again, he stared at him without saying anything, this time for just five seconds. Tobin fidgeted in his seat, his eyes wide.

"Would it surprise you to know my office checked with the FSMB to find out about you and your credentials?"

"I'm sorry, but I don't know what you're talking about."

"Well, *Mr.* Tobin, if you truly were a physician, you'd know that the FSMB is the Federation of State Medical Boards. It can tell you if a doctor has a license to practice medicine in any state in the country. And you, sir, have no license to practice medicine in any state in these United States and never have had."

"Objection, the ASA is testifying."

"Overruled. You may continue, Mr. Thomblin."

"Thank you, your honor. In fact, Mr. Tobin, you were sentenced to serve five years in the state penitentiary in the state of New York for practicing medicine in the state of New York without a license. You were just released after those five years in January 2021, were you not?"

"None of that's true," Tobin said.

Ignoring this, Thomblin said, "So, you cannot demand that I call you Dr. Tobin. I have it all right here if you'd like to see the report. I've given a copy of it to your attorney, Mr. Burns, and to Judge Redding, but I'll be happy to share it with you, if you've had a memory lapse about it. In fact, a federal marshal is prepared to arrest you on the charge of continuing to practice medicine without a license after having served in the penitentiary for that offense, so you're going back to prison on that charge regardless of what happens in this trial."

"I told you that's all a lie. I was licensed in the state of New York and I never was in a prison in my life."

"The FSMB begs to differ, Mr. Tobin. But I'll leave that matter in the hands of the federal marshal. We're here to determine what happened to Lily Kincaid on May 15."

When he next spoke, the chief assistant state attorney asked, "What time did you say Ms. Kincaid left your office?"

"It was around 8:15."

"How did she leave?"

"By the back door, since it was dark in the front of the office and I had the outdoor light on in the back."

"I don't mean by which door did she leave, I meant how did she leave?"

Tobin looked confused. "I don't know what you're asking."

"It's a simple question, doctor. Did she walk out, did she limp out using a cane, or did you carry her? How did she leave your office?"

"She walked out, of course," Tobin snapped, glaring at his attorney, wondering why he wasn't objecting to this line of questioning.

Thomblin stared at him again for a second. Then, he smiled, and said, "Did she, really?"

"Yes, I said she did," Tobin snapped again.

"I don't think you're telling me the truth," Thomblin said.

"Objection, the ASA is testifying again."

"Sustained. Please rephrase your question, Mr. Thomblin."

"Yes, your honor. Mr. Tobin . . ."

"That's Dr. Tobin," the defendant snapped again.

"Oh, pardon me, but we've already covered that territory, Mr. Tobin."

"Objection!"

"Sustained. Rephrase your question, Mr. Thomblin."

"Sorry again, your honor." To the defendant, he asked, "Did you not understand earlier when I told you about the report from the FSMB?"

"Dr. Tobin is my name and that's what you will call me," he said.

Thomblin smiled broadly for a moment, and then said, "Are you telling the truth when you say Ms. Kincaid walked out of your office and remember you've sworn to tell the truth to this court."

Tobin wiped the sweat beads off his forehead with his yellow handkerchief. He said nothing and Redding said, "Please answer the question."

All of a sudden, Tobin flushed and yelled, "Alright, alright, you want the truth? Well, here it is."

Burns sprang from his seat. "Your honor, may I have a moment with my client, please?"

"Yes, you may approach, Mr. Burns." Thomblin stepped back down to his table and consulted with his second chair as the assistant public defender talked with his client in hushed tones. After a few minutes, he threw up his hands and walked back to his seat, saying nothing to the court.

"You may answer the question now," Redding said after Burns was back in his chair, and Thomblin had stepped back up to his place in front of the defendant.

"Thank you, your honor. What I was going to say was that I did kill Lily Kincaid."

The buzzing in the courtroom got louder and members of the press rushed out the door to call their offices on their cell phones, letting the door bang behind them. The gavel came down hard. "Order! Now!"

"Thank you, Mr. Tobin. That's all I have."

"Dr. Tobin. Dr. Tobin!" the defendant yelled, to the departing back of the prosecutor.

"Mr. Burns, do you have anything else for this witness?"

"Yes, your Honor, I do, thank you." Looking at Tobin, he said, "Please, tell this court why you took the life of Lily Kincaid."

"Certainly. As you can see from that photograph of her on the easel, Lily Kincaid was a beautiful young woman. She had a right to be remembered as a beautiful young woman instead of as a dried up, wrinkled old woman who had to use a walker to get around, which she would have become one day had she lived. I gave her that gift. She will always be remembered as a beautiful young woman now, will she not?"

"Monster!" This came from the father of Lily Kincaid, on his feet now, shaking his fist at the defendant. The judge looked at the bailiff, who went to where he was standing and asked him to please sit down and not yell anything else to the defendant or he would be asked to leave the courtroom. "I don't want to have to escort you out," she said, with kindness in her manner and her voice.

He looked at the young officer and then back at the dais, and said, "I'm sorry, your honor. That won't happen again." To the bailiff, he said, "He isn't worth it. I'll sit and be quiet now. Thank you for your kindness to both of us."

The bailiff smiled and went back to her post and the courtroom was as quiet as a church during silent prayers. The judge looked at the attorney and asked, "Do you have anything else, Mr. Burns?"

"No, your honor."

"Mr. Thomblin?"

"Thank you, your honor. Mr. Tobin, do you mean to have this court believe you killed young Lily Kincaid, who had her whole life ahead of her, for altruistic reasons?"

"Yes, I do, because it's the truth."

"Tell me again exactly why you believed you needed to fill a 100 cc syringe with ethylene glycol and inject it into Lily Kincaid, please, so I can understand your reasoning."

"Oh for goodness sakes, I've already told you once."

"Answer the question as instructed, Mr. Tobin."

"Yes, your honor. Okay, Lily Kincaid was in her early twenties, and a striking young woman. I had nothing against her. Actually, I liked her very much. But, she had a right to always be that same beautiful young woman in the minds of everyone who knew her, so I made it possible that she would never grow old. That's why I killed her. It was the only way she could stay young."

Those who remained in the courtroom looked stunned, but no one said a word or murmured. Only the sound of silence prevailed until

Thomblin looked at the judge and said, "I have nothing further for this witness."

"Mr. Burns, do you have any more questions for this witness?"

With a slump to his shoulders that wasn't there earlier, Cyrus Burns said, "The Defense rests, your honor."

"You may step down, Mr. Tobin."

Tobin left the witness chair and went back to the table, where an officer was waiting to put the cuffs on him to escort him out of the courtroom and back to the jail.

"We'll be back in the courtroom promptly at 1 this afternoon. This court is adjourned for lunch." The gavel came down, all rose and the judge left for his chambers.

Tobin looked back toward the Kincaids before he was taken from the courtroom. To everyone's astonishment and disgust, he smiled broadly at the grief-stricken parents of the young woman whose life he took.

The victim's father's fists clenched tighter, but he said nothing. He didn't need to. His look said it all. He never wanted to destroy another human being as much as he wanted to destroy Alexander Tobin. For his wife's sake, he turned his back on him and took her hand. His wife looked numb and was no longer sobbing. Meggie Saurus came to them and told them to follow her to the same exit they'd taken before to avoid the crowds.

Outside on the steps of the courthouse, the reporters were questioning Sam Thomblin. Mandy Miles asked, "Mr. Thomblin, will the case go to the jury this afternoon?"

"I have no idea what the judge will do, Mandy. He might come back at 1 and instruct us to have our closing arguments ready for tomorrow morning at 9, in which case, the jury might be instructed after lunch at 1 tomorrow. I just have no idea what's in his head right now."

Miles persisted. "If the jury does get the case tomorrow afternoon, do you think they will come back quickly with a verdict, seeing as the defendant confessed right in the courtroom that he did kill Lily Kincaid?"

"I don't even want to speculate on that one. Now, if you will all excuse me, it's been a trying morning and I, for one, need to get some lunch in me. Thank you all." With that, he walked down the steps and got into the car his wife parked directly in front of the courthouse steps. He grabbed her hand when she started the car and said, "You have no idea how glad I am to see you!"

"After what I just watched on the screen, yes, I know exactly how glad you are to see me and to get back to normal. Try to put that monster out of your mind for a couple hours and let's have a nice quiet lunch. I have it all prepared at home. I don't think you want to go out to eat after that insanity in there."

"You're exactly what I need and all I need for the next two hours. Yes, let's please go home to eat so I can slough that testimony out of my head for now. I love you, Lola Bridger-Thomblin. So very much. You're the most beautiful, the most wonderful woman in this world and you're perfect for me." He kissed her hand.

"And you, my handsome debonair husband, are so perfect for me, and I love you with my entire being. Is that wonderful enough for you?" She was grinning and her husband smiled, knowing she was never one to splurge on the superlatives about him, and leaned his head back, contented, on the seat as she continued to drive them to their little island hideaway on the beach off Sugarloaf Key, fourteen miles north of Key West, where they could always shut out the world they both lived in at work and where the evil they had to contend with day after day could never penetrate their own private paradise.

NINETEEN

"All rise. The Honorable Judge Clinton Redding presiding." The judge asked everyone to sit, including the bailiff, so she took her seat at the side of the courtroom.

"Mr. Burns are you ready to give your closing argument?"

"Yes, I am, your honor." He arose from his seat at the table and walked over to stand before the jury. He did not speak immediately, but stood silently looking at the jurors. "Ladies and Gentlemen, the prosecutor painted a beautiful picture of the victim during this trial. Well, let me tell you there are two victims in this trial and one of them is the defendant, Alexander Tobin. I suppose everything we've heard about Ms. Kincaid is true, and my sincere condolences go to her parents. Dr. Tobin even admitted he liked her very much. But we're not here to talk about what a wonderful young woman Ms. Kincaid was. We're here to decide the fate of that young man sitting at the defense table. Did he pretend to be a doctor when in fact he is not one? Yes, the facts speak for themselves. But by his own admission, he cared so much about his patients that he accommodated them no matter how late or how early they needed to see him. And truthfully, you aren't here to do anything about whether Alex Tobin was a real doctor or a fake doctor. You're here to decide his guilt or innocence and to follow the instructions of the judge when he turns the case over to you. There is much about Mr.

Tobin's early life that you are not aware of and that might have been a factor in why he did what he did, but I cannot tell you about them, because I must follow the rules of a courtroom trial and cannot speak about anything that has not been brought into evidence. In retrospect, perhaps I should have pushed harder to have them presented to this court so you could consider them."

Burns continued, after looking back at his client for a few moments. "I want you to deliberate carefully and thoroughly. Afterward, I want you to render a verdict of not guilty, so this does not follow this young man for the rest of his life. Thank you and thank you for your service to this community by serving on this jury."

Judge Redding said, "Thank you, Mr. Burns, and asked, "Mr. Thomblin, are you ready to give your closing argument?"

"Yes, I am, your honor." He walked to stand in front of the jury. Like Burns, he did not speak for several more minutes. When he did Meggie Saurus thought it was one of his best closing arguments. "Ladies and Gentlemen, thank you for fulfilling your civic duty to listen intently to the case before you and to be willing to render your verdict after careful deliberation. We already know, by his own admission in this court, that Alexander Tobin is the killer of Lily Kincaid, a young woman barely out of her teens who had her entire life ahead of her. I don't know what she'd planned for her future to be, but," and he pointed to the defendant, "that man, Alexander Tobin, who pretended to be a physician, decided to play God with that young woman's life. He tries to make us believe he was being altruistic, that he just wanted to spare her the life of an elderly woman with wrinkles and liver spots and poor mobility. He wants us to believe he was being kind to Lily Kincaid, the young librarian whom he claimed to have liked very much. Do people who like other people very much kill them without a second thought? I'll let you be the judge of that.

"Ladies and gentlemen, I want you to listen very carefully to Judge Redding's instructions and to deliberate over the facts of this case just as carefully. And after you've done that, I want you to return a verdict of first degree murder against this man who pretended to be a physician for the sole purpose of, from his own testimony, killing someone like

Lily Kincaid. Thank you for your service to this community today and every day of this trial. "

"Thank you, Mr. Thomblin." Judge Redding removed his glasses and rubbed his eyes for a moment and then he looked at the jury. "Ladies and gentlemen of the jury, I will dismiss you now and at five this evening, you will be driven by a member of this court to be sequestered in a hotel where you will eat, sleep and return every evening until such time as you've rendered a verdict in this case. I urge you to take all of the facts you've heard in this courtroom into your minds and only deliberate upon them, not anything else you might have heard outside this courtroom. You will each have a room by yourself in the hotel, so you will have your privacy during your sequestration. Do not discuss the case with anyone, including each other, except when you are in the jury room. Do not watch television news and do not read a newspaper until after you've finished the work you're here to do. If you have any questions or want to see a particular piece of evidence again, your foreman will step out into the hall and ask the bailiff to bring it to you. Your lunch will be brought to you in the jury room so you will not have to go anywhere but there when you are taken from the hotel. The verdicts you must consider are: number one, guilty of murder in the first degree, which means the murder was planned by the defendant; number two, guilty of murder in the second degree – not a planned murder, but a crime of passion not thought of until that moment – and number three, not guilty by reason of insanity. If you believe it is number three, we'll accept your verdict and as is required before sentencing, we will have a pre-sentence investigation and that will include the testimony of two court-appointed psychiatrists who will give us their expert opinion after they each examine Mr. Tobin. You may go back to the jury room now and begin deliberations until five o'clock, which I realize is just two hours from now. Thank you for your service to our community by serving on this jury. Everyone, please remain seated until the jury has left this room."

He waited until each juror had passed through the door, brought down his gavel and said, "This court is adjourned."

Both Burns and Thomblin moved toward each other and shook hands. Meggie Saurus walked back to escort the Kincaids out the side exit, and then the assistant state attorneys and assistant public defenders started gathering their papers into their proper folders and put them into their briefcases. Each chief was bombarded by the press and the media as soon as they reached the courthouse steps, and answered their questions with, "We'll all have to wait to see what the jury brings back to the courtroom."

TWENTY

On day three of sequestration, the jury had still not decided upon a verdict. The foreman, Chet Anthony, a local firefighter, said to the eleven other jurors, "Look, I know everyone's tired of this, but I think we owe it to that woman's parents to bring in a verdict soon. Okay?" No one spoke but everyone nodded in agreement. "One more time, let's go around the table and with raised hands answer the questions. How many for guilty of first degree murder?" Only four hands went up. He ran his hands through his thick dark brown hair and rolled his head on his neck a couple of times. "Alright, how many for guilty of second degree murder?" No hands went up. "Innocent by reason of insanity?" Seven hands went into the air.

"Chet," Mary Lou Harper said, "I think we're all just too tired to think about this anymore, this evening. It's ten till five already. Let's just gather our things and knock on the door for the bailiff to get our driver. I, for one, need a quiet space and a hot soothing bath before dinner comes to my door."

Admitting defeat to himself, Anthony said, "You're right, Mary Lou. I'm beat, too, so let's just call it a day – again – and get back to the hotel for the night. Maybe after a good night's sleep, we'll all be of one accord and decide that guilty means guilty. He grabbed his backpack and knocked on the door.

It was the beginning of day four in the jury room. As before, Anthony called for a vote. This time nine hands including his went up for guilty of first degree murder. "That's more like it," he said, with a relieved smile. "Would the three of you who are still for innocent by reason of insanity care to share why you still believe this? Remember, the judge already has indicated that he will do the sentencing, that we are excused from that responsibility. Also, that the court-appointed psychiatrists are going to examine Tobin during presentencing investigation, so if we say he is guilty of first degree murder, but both of them say he is too mentally ill to have committed first degree murder, the judge has the prerogative to sentence him to life in a mental institution. I say we leave that up to the psychiatrists and the judge and just vote on the evidence."

Murmuring went around the table. Jason Worth, who owned the largest hardware store on the island, said, "I don't know, Chet. We were given innocent by reason of insanity as one of our choices. I'm sticking to that. I'm sorry. How about you, Beth and Jack?" Beth Harding was a fifth grade teacher and eager to get back to her students. Jack Dooley, a widowed retired engineer, was just as eager to get packing for his trip to see his elderly parents in Wisconsin. He'd planned it long before the trial started and was disappointed, as were his parents, when he was called to jury duty. He'd never minded before, but his parents were both frail and he was anxious about their health. The other two said nothing, just looked down at the table.

"Let's just vote again, Chet, and see what happens this time. We sure don't want a hung jury so the judge will have no recourse but to ask us to go back and try again or dismiss the charges against that monster, as the victim's dad called him and I don't blame him."

That statement sounded optimistic to Anthony. Is Jack going to cave, after all? Will the others? "Okay, it's headed toward three, so let's do this. Let's call for coffee and a snack so we'll all be a little more alert for the late hour and then we'll have another vote. How does that sound?"

Everyone agreed they could use a break, so he knocked on the door again. The bailiff brought back a large tray filled with cheese, crackers and Danish pastries. Behind her was another officer with a large carafe of coffee. "Yeah, this looks more like it. Thanks, officers, we appreciate this," he told them. Others nodded in agreement.

"Our pleasure," they both said, and left them to it. They took their time with the snacks and each had two cups of coffee before they decided that, since it was nearing four, maybe they'd better try another vote.

"Okay then," Anthony said to the group of sated jurors, "let's clear the table and this time we'll vote by secret ballot." Lila Smith, another retiree, gathered up all the paper plates and utensils and put them back on the large tray, and picked it up. Anthony picked up the coffee carafe and knocked on the door for the bailiff. After she took the tray and the other officer took the carafe, he closed the door and they each took a slip of paper from the center of the table. Everyone wrote their verdict on it and put it into the woven basket Anthony passed around.

"Okay, that's everyone. Let's see what we have," he said, glancing at the clock and seeing it was a quarter till four. "First degree, first degree, first degree, first degree, first degree, first degree, first degree, first degree, first degree, first degree, innocent by reason of insanity, first degree." He sighed, but smiled at the group and said, "We might have to spend another night at the hotel, but we're closer to a verdict, so we've made progress."

"Progress but no checkered flag, "Jackie Clements, a former race car driver, said. He threw his pen on the table and slumped back down in his seat. His wife had just had their third child before the trial started and he just wanted to be home with her and their family.

"Hey, I'm as disappointed as anyone, Jackie, but we're much better off than we were this morning. Now, I'm not going to ask who voted innocent by reason of insanity. What I am going to do," he said, looking at the clock, "is ask for one more vote before we call it a day. I'm not giving up and going back in there and tell the judge we're a hung jury. I don't want that guy free to walk the streets again and I don't think any of the rest of you want it, either." Anthony picked up the small tray of the blank note paper and handed one to each of them.

They were all feeling the exhaustion by then and wanted to get this over with so they could go home to their families or if they had none, at least to their own bed and dinner table. None of them believed they were going to come to an agreement on a verdict before five o'clock.

"Okay, you've all got your ballot so let's vote." Anthony looked around the table at his tired fellow jurors. He was glad no tempers had gotten out of hand as he'd heard of with other juries. Jackie wasn't throwing a tantrum about it, either; he just wanted to get back to Gloria, his new baby and her sister and brother. He didn't blame him one bit. He hadn't even gotten to take her home from the hospital but had to call her brother and his wife to drive down from West Palm to pick her and the baby up. They'd gone a step further and offered to stay with them until Jackie was free to be home with them. Anthony would have felt the same way had it been him.

Everyone was through and had put their notes into the basket at four-thirty. "Well," he said with an anxious smile, "here goes. Guilty first degree, first degree, first degree . . ." When he'd read every ballot, there were twelve guilty in the first degree. They were all smiling and looking as relieved as people who'd just been told they were paroled from prison, rather than twelve people who were potentially sending Tobin to prison. "Any doubts about your vote?" he asked. Everyone shook their heads no. Anthony knocked on the door and told the bailiff they were ready to go back to court. She told them to relax and she'd come back to get them when the judge was back in the courtroom. It was now four forty-five.

~ ~ ~

"All rise. The honorable Clinton Redding presiding." The bailiff was almost smiling as she said it. Like everyone else, she was relieved or at least hoped there was no hung jury, although she'd have to wait like everyone else to know this.

"Please be seated. This court is now in session. Bailiff, please bring in the jury," Redding said, sounding tired but relieved, too. The jury had waited until five-thirty, because all of the attorneys, the family of the victim, reporters, witnesses who were now free to be in the courtroom as spectators and others did not come back to court all at once. But they were all there now, so it wouldn't be long until everyone could go home and the jurors could go back to their own homes for the first time in days.

As the twelve men and women walked into the courtroom one at a time and quickly took their seats, every eye was glued to them, wondering if they'd reached a verdict or were a hung jury. When they were all seated, the judge asked, "Mr. Foreman, have you reached a verdict?"

Anthony said, "We have, your honor."

"Bailiff, please bring the verdict to me." He watched her walk to Chet Anthony and he handed her the paper with the verdict hand-written on it. She in turn walked to the dais and handed it to the judge. He looked at it, but his expression did not tell those watching what was on the paper. He handed it back to the bailiff.

"Will the defendant please rise. I want silence in this courtroom while the verdict is read by the foreman," the judge said to the spectators in the large courtroom he knew he'd never preside over again. "Mr. Foreman, please read the verdict."

"We find the defendant, Alexander Tobin, guilty of murder in the first degree," Anthony read.

"Is this the unanimous decision of this jury?" Anthony told him it was. "As is my practice, I am going to poll the jury. As I call your number, please tell me if you voted yes." He polled the twelve by number and they all said yes.

"Alexander Tobin, you've been found guilty, by a jury of your peers, of premeditated murder in the first degree of Lily Kincaid. I am remanding you to jail until such time as your presentencing investigation is completed and sentence is pronounced upon you. At that time, you will be asked if you wish to speak. Not this time. In a few minutes the officers will take you back to your cell at the jail. Two officers continued to stand behind Alexander Tobin. They were there for his protection, as well as to guard that he didn't try to get away, and to remove him from the courtroom when the judge instructed. One of them did ask him quietly to put his hands behind his back. He did so, without protest, and was cuffed. Another person stood in back of the two officers to follow the three of them out. He was a federal marshal, but no one knew that except Sam Thomblin, Cyrus Burns and Judge Redding.

The courtroom was silent. No one moved toward the doors. Not even the reporters. Everyone sensed the judge still had something important to say, because he did not dismiss the jury right away as was his practice and the practice of most other judges. Instead, he looked at each one of them and then looked out at all the spectators in this large courtroom where he'd spent the past thirty years of his life and wondered where all those years went.

"Officers, please escort the prisoner back to the county jail. Thank you." The officers motioned for Tobin to stand and one lead him out while the other one followed them. The federal marshall followed behind all of them before the judge adjourned.

Redding cleared his throat and turned to the jury, "Ladies and gentlemen of this jury, thank you so much for your service to this community throughout this trial and for your honest and difficult hard work to reach a verdict in this case. You are hereby dismissed and free to speak of this case to whomever you wish without consequence from this court. Godspeed."

As the reporters hurried through the doors, banging them as usual, the judge looked over toward them and smiled, knowing he would never hear that sound again from this bench. "This court is dismissed," he said, and lowered his gavel for the last time. He hurried from the courtroom.

Several spectators gathered around the Kincaids, wishing them peace, not well, as they knew wishing them well under the circumstances of their daughter's killer being found guilty was a useless expression. They wanted them to have some peace about it, though, so they did not hesitate to say it to them. Many who knew them intimately expressed their willingness to listen if they wanted to call in the middle of the night or any other time, or to visit if they wished to see them. They told all of them thanks and walked out of the courtroom's side entrance with the assistant state attorney, as before. They just wanted to get home where they could sit and cry all day if they wanted to, away from others' eyes and well-meaning words. They could not fathom finding peace over their precious Lily's death. All they wanted in this world was to have her back, alive and well, laughing and talking with them again. They had no idea how they were going to face another day without her, much less the rest of their lives without having her presence fill their existence. How do other parents do it? How does anyone do it? They had no answers. It was what it was – a vast existence of emptiness. They knew it would always be so.

TWENTY-ONE

Maggie Metronia, sitting there in the courtroom with her two Key West family members, was one of those who wondered if that hesitation to speak was the judge's silent swan song to them all. The three of them had planned to go to dinner in the garden of La Te Da after the end of the trial this evening, and she didn't want to bring them down with any sad note about the judge or anything else, though she supposed the end of the trial would be all anyone else would be talking about, and if it came up with her companions, she wouldn't hush them.

As suspected, the garden was crowded, but they asked for a table for three, despite the crowd. As they were escorted to a table toward the back, they nodded, smiled and spoke to some friendly acquaintances. Soon they were seated and had ordered their drinks, cups of tea for the two ladies and Sam Adams for Homer. The waitress was back with them in mere minutes.

With her usual friendly smile, she asked, "Are you ready to order or do you need a while?"

Knowing what they wanted since they'd eaten there often, Homer gave her their orders, "our usuals, please." She smiled and picked up their menus and left them with their drinks.

As Carolyn stirred the stevia into her simmering Earl Grey, she said, "I don't know about either of you, but I felt like Judge Redding was doing more than just adjourning court."

Homer asked, "Oh? What did you think he was doing, Caro?" He smiled lazily at her and then turned up his bottle for another long draw.

"I thought he was saying farewell to us, didn't you? How about you, Maggie? Did you feel the same way?" She took a sip of her tea while looking at her friends. A rooster wandered through the garden and she smiled down at him. Someone else who apparently didn't know how the chickens were tolerated everywhere on the island by almost every local took both hands and shooed the rooster toward the outside. He stood his ground and scurried away from the offending patron, as he continued to strut among the patrons before he got tired of getting no handouts and left the garden.

"Yes, I have to admit I felt he was saying goodbye – to the bench, at least. Since he was born and bred on the island, I don't see him ever leaving. But, yes, hanging up his robe and calling it a day seemed to be exactly what Judge Redding was doing as he looked out at the courtroom and then hesitated before speaking to the jury. I won't be surprised to hear that he will retire after he sentences Tobin, if not before. After all, any judge familiar with the case can impose sentence after the pre-sentencing investigation, so he wouldn't necessarily have to hang around for that."

Their steaming hot food came at the moment Maggie finished speaking, as though the waitress had hung back for a moment to let her finish speaking. "Here you go, folks. Steak for Homer, salmon for Carolyn and yellowtail for Ms. Maggie," she said with a flourish and a smile.

Maggie patted her hand. "Simone, you always know without our saying it what we're going to order and you make sure it's prepared perfectly."

The waitress laughed and said, "Well, I think Chef has more to do with its being prepared perfectly, but yes, I always have a pretty good idea what the three of you are having but for dinner, only. When you come to lunch, I've noticed you always seem to try a different dish every time, so I don't venture a guess on that. Well, if you'll excuse me, I have a full house to serve, so I'll leave and let you eat. Bon appetit."

After they finished dinner with no dessert, since Maggie had a huge Key Lime Pie waiting for them at home, they strolled slowly back up Duval to United. It was still a thrill for Maggie to come upon the beautiful historic home she bought with some of her Powerball winnings. Sometimes it was difficult for her to believe it really was her home and no one could take it away from her. It was gleaming white in tonight's sunset with reds and golden spears of color splayed over it, highlighting the bright red of the house's shutters. She let out a deep breath as Homer opened the gate for them. Home. It meant so much to her after her more austere beginnings on this island.

They no sooner were in the house when Maggie's cell rang. "Yes?"

Chief Doan said, "Maggie, your speedy trial has been scheduled for tomorrow at 9, so don't be late. The judge said we will meet in the conference room as we did for your other hearings."

"Oh," she told him.

"Anything wrong? Do you have other plans?"

"No, Chief, I'll be there bright and early," she said, not without trepidation creeping up her spine. "Okay, goodbye now."

"Goodbye, Maggie. Oh by the way, the judge said he's considering passing sentence shortly after the verdict is rendered." He disconnected with a grin she couldn't see.

"How can he do that? I've been to a lot of trials on this island and there's never once been a sentencing afterward."

"What was that all about, Mag?"

"Well, " she said, "they're just now getting around to the trial and it's going to be held tomorrow at 9 in the same conference room we were in before, plus the judge told Lenny he's thinking of passing sentence on me soon after the verdict is rendered."

Trying very hard not to give the truth away to her, he said, "Well, don't you worry, now, because we'll both be right there with you and whatever comes, we'll get through it together." Carolyn nodded with him.

"That's a sweet sentiment, my friends, but if I go to jail or worse to prison, neither of you can follow, so in that case I'm afraid there's no possibility of us getting through it together. I'll be on my own to take whatever comes."

She sighed and walked into the kitchen, being stunned as always when she looked at the large portrait of Homer and her in the foyer. If only life were as it was then, so carefree, smiling at the world. She bit her lower lip, wishing for just a moment that she had the courage to get those implants, as Homer and Carolyn begged her to let Dr. Troxel put into her mouth so she could have her smile back. It was a beautiful smile, she admitted to herself, without a trace of vanity.

Over pie and decaf, Carolyn said, "I still wonder why they're holding either of your meetings in the conference room and mostly I wonder why you'd go there without an attorney again." Her arraignment had followed quickly on the heels of her bond hearing so she knew it was the trial next and who holds a trial in a conference room? Nothing seemed fair in their treatment of Maggie.

Maggie said nothing. Homer spoke up then and said, "I really think he's going to go easy on her, Carolyn. Maggie, I think he's going to give you community service since you have no criminal record of any kind."

She answered him on another big sigh. "I wish I had your confidence about it, my friend. Would one of you put all this away, please? I feel tired all of a sudden and think I'll turn in early for a change."

"I'll clean everything up, dear." She put her arm around Maggie's shoulders and added, "I feel good about tomorrow. I think Homer's right. I see a certain number of hours doing good for the community in your immediate future, dear soul. Don't you give it another thought, now, and just get a nice long soak in that beautiful big claw-footed tub of yours and go to bed. We'll both be right there with you in the morning, so you don't have to face it alone. Goodnight." She squeezed her shoulders and kissed her on the cheek.

"Carolyn's right. You just need to relax in a good long tub bath and go to bed. We have your back in the morning." He hugged her and kissed the top of her head.

She said nothing as she smiled at them and then turned toward her bedroom at the front of the house. She didn't bother drawing a bath. She was simply too tired, an exhaustion she rarely, if ever felt. She was nowhere near 80, but for the first time in her life, she felt old. Used up. No use to society.

She sighed and changed into her nightgown before lying down under the sheets and duvet. She was asleep within five minutes. The sunset had disappeared from the sky just moments before and she didn't stir as night shadows drifted around her from the trees and bushes outside her bedroom window. A lone rooster crowed, as roosters did at any and all hours on the lovely island home she loved with all her being.

TWENTY-TWO

Two things were on the minds of most Key Westers that morning. First, as so many suspected, this morning's paper bore the headline, "Respected and beloved judge retires" and secondly, word, as it so often does there, got around the little two by four mile island of Key West that Maggie Metronia's trial was starting this morning. Word also said since it was not a trial by jury, it would be the judge who will render a verdict and sentence her soon after, possibly sending her to jail to await prison. No one knew when the Coconut Telegraph originated. Possibly it had existed since there was a Key West, but every local knew it was the most accurate newscaster on the island.

When the three of them, Maggie, Homer and Carolyn arrived at the courthouse, the little island city had turned out in force. Signs proclaiming Maggie's innocence were everywhere they looked, bringing tears to her eyes. She knew nearly everyone in the little city of less than thirty thousand, by sight if not by name, but never knew she was so well liked, even loved, if those signs and shouts were any indication.

They walked into the courthouse and started to go back to the small conference room when the bailiff stopped them. "You'll be in the courtroom this morning, after all, Ms. Maggie," she told her. "In the meanwhile, I'm to take you back to the little room where Annette Bailey, is waiting." Bailey was Maggie's attorney.

Carolyn and Homer started to follow, but she beckoned them to remain in the courtroom. "Well, that's different," Homer said. "They've asked us to be there the other times."

"Well, Ms. Bailey wasn't there the other times and what's between Maggie and her attorney *is* privileged, Homer, so don't be insulted. Thank heavens she has one this time."

"You're right and I'm grateful she doesn't have to go through this without a good lawyer. Have you met Annette Bailey?"

"No," she answered, "I've heard you and Maggie mention her, but we've never met and I don't know everyone there is to know on this island, either. She's probably a good attorney or Maggie wouldn't have her on retainer."

"You're right about that. Annette has been there for Mag ever since she won Powerball all those years ago and she's never steered her wrong. She's almost as old as Maggie is, but is still sharp as a tack."

"That's interesting. I'm surprised she's working this long," Carolyn said. "Most women would be retired long before they reach her age. But more power to her if she is able to work and still enjoys the job."

"She does enjoy it," Homer told her, with a smile.

They found the only two vacant seats near the front. The courthouse was packed with people supporting their friend. Maggie didn't know a lot of people by name, but she always acknowledged familiar faces and even those she'd never seen before. People liked to be recognized. In that respect she had a lot of friends and every one of them must have turned out for her trial.

Soon, the door opened and a tall attractive woman with café a lait complexion and dark auburn hair streaked with silver led Maggie to the defense table. She glanced back to see where her friends were and spying them in the second row from where she sat relieved her mind. She gave them a small smile and then turned her attention to what Bailey was saying to her.

"All rise! This court is in session. The Honorable Scott T. Fitzgerald presiding! Some in the spectator seats smiled at the name as they always did when hearing Judge Fitzgerald's name. Others who didn't read books had no clue.

"You may be seated," the judge told them, as Maggie wondered why Judge Lopez wasn't presiding over her trial since he'd been there for her bond hearing and arraignment. They noisily took their seats and then there was silence. "I'm sure you all are expecting a certain forum and decorum this morning, but this will be a bit different from any trial procedure you're used to."

He let that sink in and continued. "I'm sure those of you who attend public meetings like the city commission meetings, in which members of the public – you – are given three minutes each to make any public statement you wish to make regarding the items on the agenda or any other pertinent subject about which you wish to make your thoughts known. Well, this morning will be no different."

People were looking at each other, puzzled as to what this could mean, when the judge continued. "Now, since no one knew about this until now, we don't have a list of you who wish to speak, as we would had you been at a city commission meeting, so I'm going to ask that if you have anything to say before this morning's trial of Ms. Maggie Metronia, you line up on the left wall of the courtroom now. And since this is a public trial, everyone who lines up will be sworn in as character witnesses for the defendant, Ms. Metronia. No one will need to come to the witness box, as we have a podium set up there on the floor before the bench."

There was a noisy scraping of shoes and seats raising to their original vertical positions as many people stood and went to the wall to line up. Maggie had turned her head at one point and was touched that so many of her fellow Key Westers had something to say about her. She hoped it was all going to be positive. "Bailiff, please swear in the witnesses," Judge Fitzgerald said, startling her and she turned back to the front and stared ahead. Since there were so many of them, this took considerable time, but finally, the bailiff finished the last person in the line, took the Bible back to the front of the courtroom and placed it on the small table before taking her place again at the other side of the room.

Indeed it was positive. For the next two hours, locals came to the podium to speak of Maggie and her kindness to them over the years. They related story after story of some small deed she'd voluntarily done to make their lives better, especially noting the extra-large tips she gave every service worker on the island who served her after she won Powerball, some so generous she even made it possible for them to pay their portion of the rent in shared housing entirely out of their tips. Some said she didn't even look at how much she was giving them, just reached into her pocket or purse and pulled out a stack of bills, many of them hundreds. City commissioners spoke of her civic mindedness and how she never missed a city commission meeting and often spoke up about what was bothering her about the city and how they took her comments seriously and often acted upon them. Members and the pastor of her little community church spoke of her volunteerism in doing different tasks during the service and of her showing up every Saturday to help cook, serve or box up hot meals for shut-ins and those who were homeless, often bringing in several of her famous homemade key lime pies to add to the lunches. Others spoke of how she volunteered to help with fundraisers for different non-profits who were holding events in the island city to benefit those less fortunate.

At the end of the two hours, the judge said he would allow those still standing to voice their comments, but immediately after that the trial would begin. Maggie began to feel anxious at that point. She'd been humbled and relaxed during the public comments before Judge Fitzgerald said he was pulling the plug on them, or that was what she thought he was doing when he interrupted them. She was happy she was wrong, that he was allowing them to speak.

"All right, Mr. Thomblin, are you ready to present your case? Adding to the unconventional way this trial will be conducted, we are going to forego opening statements this morning."

"Thank you, your honor, I am. I call Leonard Doan, Key West Police Department Chief."

Doan came in through the doors and went to the witness box. Before being seated, he was sworn in by the bailiff. As was his practice, he was dressed in his impeccable uniform rather than street clothing and made quite the impression, as always.

After he took his seat, the prosecutor went to stand in front of him. He was dressed as casually as decorum allowed on the island, in dark gray trousers, dark gray loafers with light blue socks, light blue shirt tucked into the pants, a dark blue and gray patterned tie and a darker blue belt completed the casual outfit. "Good morning, Chief Doan," he said and the chief responded in kind.

"On the evening of May 15, 2021, do you recall where you were and why you were there?"

"Sure," replied the chief, "My men and I were at the home of whom we thought then was a local doctor, Alexander Tobin."

"And why were you at Mr. Tobin's home that particular night?"

"We'd been told by two residents that they witnessed the doctor putting a long needle into the back of the neck of a young woman, causing her to lose consciousness almost immediately."

"In fact, these two residents believe the doctor had killed this young woman, correct?"

"Yes, sir, that's correct."

"Can you identify the two witnesses at this time?"

"Yes, one was Maggie Metronia, seated at the defense table, and the other one was Carolyn Cramer, seated in the third row of the courtroom." Both women flushed when he mentioned their names.

"Thank you, chief. Can you describe what you found as you pulled up in front of Alexander Tobin's home?"

"Certainly. Every light in the house was turned on when we arrived. I'd asked the men to stand down until we were ready to arrest Mr. Tobin. As I approached the house, I saw a movement by the shrubbery to the south side of the house."

"And was that movement Mr. Tobin?"

The chief smiled and said, "No, it was Maggie, er Maggie Metronia. I'd noticed her red trike first and knew she was hiding somewhere."

"Was this unusual, chief? That you'd find her at the scene when you arrived?"

He smiled again and answered, "No, Maggie was often at the scene or near the scene. She seemed to have a sixth sense of when we needed to apprehend someone."

"What did you say to her, if anything?"

"I ordered her to go home, that she shouldn't be there, that we were trying to apprehend a suspect."

"What was her reaction to that order?"

"She told me she'd leave, but before she did, she said the subject, Mr. Tobin, was on the other side of the house, pacing in another room with windows for walls as in the rest of the house."

"And was this true?"

"Oh yes, he was there and he was pacing back and forth."

"What happened after she told you this?"

"Well, I thought she went home, as she got on her trike and left as I'd told her to do."

"You *thought* she went home? Is this court to believe by this statement that she did not go home?"

"That's right. After the subject got away from all of us, because he'd sprayed himself all over with cooking oil and literally slipped right through our fingers, we ran out of the house after him and I yelled that he was going to his boat docked across the street."

"And then what happened?"

"We all ran to the dock and someone tripped over an adult trike, a bright red one like I knew Maggie rode."

"What did that tell you?"

"That she had not gone home but doubled back and had gotten on the subject's boat before we got to it."

"Did you get her off the boat at that point?"

"No, we didn't have a chance to because Tobin had already started the engine and the boat was moving away from the dock. We couldn't see Maggie on it, but knew she had to be there because she wasn't anywhere else on the property or across the street by the dock."

"What kind of problem did this present to you and your men, Chief? Or did it?"

"Oh yes, it presented a serious dilemma for us. Had she not been on the boat, we would have fired on it at the subject and tried to disable him from leaving the dock or at least taken him down, so we could jump into the boat right away after we caught up with him in our squad boat."

"So, let me understand why this was such a problem. Take me through what course of action you took instead of firing at him from your boat."

"Well, we had to sneak up on him in our police boat and two of our men had to climb aboard his boat to try to apprehend him before he could get away from us. They were able to do this, but not knowing where on the boat Maggie was hiding, they couldn't just randomly fire at the suspect."

"Okay, so now they're on the boat, sneaking up on him, is that correct?"

"Yes, they were trying to, but he heard them and fired his gun at them. He apparently had placed it on the seat to the side of the wheel before he started the boat. When they kept coming, he left the wheel and actively engaged in a gunfight with the two officers."

"And where was Ms. Metronia while this was going on?"

"We could not see her anywhere on the boat, until at one point she stood up beside the gunwale in back of the subject and walked quickly to the bow."

"What was her reason for doing that? Or did you know why?"

"We didn't at first, but then it was obvious she was going to try to take the wheel. You see without anyone steering the boat, it was more or less going around in circles and coming very close to our police boat, but we had to stay close enough to his to jump aboard to help the other officers."

"And were you able to do this?"

"Yes, when we saw that he was moving further into the stern of his boat, we were able to get in front and behind him. Blake Butler, my lieutenant, got in front of him, taunting him to keep his attention riveted to the stern so I could get behind him and up to the wheel to take it from Maggie."

"Oh, so she was unable to get control of it, then, after she grabbed the wheel?"

"No, she eventually got it to straighten out. Had she not, if it did strike our boat, there very well could have been an explosion, but I took it from her, anyway, and told her to get down. She balked first, saying she had it covered, but I insisted it was an order and she let go of the wheel and got down out of sight."

"Did Mr. Tobin ever see the two of you back at the bow?"

"Yes, he turned at one point and fired a shot but then one of our officers was able to grab his gun and they put him in cuffs. At the same time, Maggie stood up and said she'd take the wheel again if I needed to help them."

"So, you relinquished the wheel back to her and went to the stern to help subdue Mr. Tobin?"

"No, when she stood, I snapped cuffs on her and one of my men came to relieve me at the wheel as the others got Tobin into the police boat."

"Help this court to understand why you took this action against the defendant."

"Maggie had gotten involved with our investigations a time or two before this and it was pretty harmless, but she went too far this time. Her actions, specifically getting into the boat instead of going home as I'd told her to do, directly hindered our disabling the suspect in order to keep him from getting away. As a result of this, since our men had to climb into his boat while he was still not disabled directly endangered their lives from his having a gun and engaging in a shooting match with them."

"I understand. No more questions of this witness, your Honor."

"Ms. Bailey, any questions for this witness before he steps down?"

"Yes, your Honor, I have just a couple of questions." She walked to stand in front of the chief. "Good morning, Chief Doan." He said good morning back to her.

"Chief, during this shootout, which sounded like it was pretty rough for a while, was anyone from the Key West Police Department injured?"

"No, ma'am, fortunately, we had no injuries."

"Was the defendant injured?"

"No, thankfully, she wasn't."

"No further questions, your Honor."

"Thank you, Ms. Bailey. Please call your next witness, Mr. Thomblin."

"Your Honor, the only other witness I had on my list was the defendant, but as you indicated to Ms. Bailey and me before we started, you wish to examine her, so I relinquish the examination to you at this time."

"Thank you, Mr. Thomblin, and thank you, Ms. Bailey, for allowing me this latitude with the defendant. Ms. Metronia, will you please come to the witness box and be sworn in."

Maggie did not know Judge Fitzgerald personally as she had Judge Redding and this turn of events scared her more than anything else had to this point. She did not know why the judge would want to question her instead of letting Mr. Thomblin do it. Surely this would not bode well for her. In their seats, Carolyn and Homer looked at each other in apprehension about this, too.

After the bailiff swore Maggie in, she had her take her seat and as before, to sit close to the microphone so she could be heard. "Good morning, Ms. Metronia."

"Good morning, your Honor."

"Before I begin my questioning, may I ask if you'd prefer to be called Maggie instead of my being so formal?"

"Yes, sir, I'd prefer it, if you don't mind."

"I don't mind at all. This is a little less formal a trial than most so I'd like to be less formal with you, as well. Now, Ms. Maggie, will you state your whole name and address for me, please."

In a quiet voice, Maggie did as the judge requested. And then she turned pale and the judge stopped for a moment and asked the bailiff to get her a drink of water. To her, he asked, "Are you okay, Ms. Maggie?"

"Yes, your honor. I just got a little woozy there for a moment. Thank you," she said to the bailiff, as she handed her the water.

Judge Fitzgerald gave her a few minutes. When her color returned, he asked, "Are you ready to begin?"

"Yes, your honor, I am."

"Okay then."

TWENTY-THREE

Ms. Maggie, please explain to this court why you got on a boat belonging to someone you knew killed another human being?"

Maggie twisted the bottom of her pale yellow three-quarter sleeved cotton top, as she always did when she was anxious about something. At first she swallowed and tried to speak but nothing came out. Her normally big blue eyes widened and her breaths were coming in exaggerated intervals. Carolyn looked at Homer and whispered, "Poor dear, she's so scared."

"I know," he whispered back. "She's pale as a ghost, again."

"Ms. Maggie, did you hear my question? Do you need another drink of water?"

She still couldn't speak, but nodded her head yes, that she did.

The bailiff, poured her another glass of the icy water from the carafe and she drank it down like a sailor, lost at sea, suddenly coming upon someone in a life raft with a gallon of refrigerated water to drink.

"Now, you thought you were better before, but are you really? We can do a continuance if you're not well." The judge understood her anxiety about being questioned by him. But they had to follow through with this for her own good.

"Yes, your Honor, I'm sorry. I can do this. Would you repeat the question, please?"

"Sure, I asked why you got on a boat belonging to someone you knew killed another human being?"

"Your Honor, I wish I knew the answer to that," she said in a quiet voice. "All I know is I didn't want him to get away from the police."

"But how did you think you could stop him? Did you have a gun or a knife or any other kind of weapon?"

"No, your Honor, I didn't. And when I got on the boat and hid by the gunwale, I had those exact same thoughts – how did I think I could have stopped him from getting away – so I just stayed hidden before he came on the boat."

"Well, thank goodness, you did or you might have been thrown off the boat and become another of his victims if he'd seen you."

"I know, your Honor. I just wasn't thinking rationally."

"Maggie Metronia, I think you have a good heart, but sometimes you let it rule your head and that's how you get yourself into these messes."

Maggie said nothing, just nodded her head at Judge Fitzgerald. Her yellow top was a mess of wrinkles now at the bottom and she had a thin bead of sweat on her forehead.

"I'm not going to ask you to answer any more questions about what you did on May 15, Ms. Maggie. Instead, I'm going to let you go back to your seat at the defense table and I'm going to go to my chambers with Ms. Bailey and Mr. Thomblin, if Ms. Bailey is willing to forego presenting her case" The defense attorney said yes, she was willing, so he continued. "After I've spoken with them, I'll be ready to render my verdict and will sentence you immediately so you won't have to wait any longer. Go now and wait for me to return to the bench."

"Yes, your Honor." She thought her legs weren't going to hold her up as she walked from the dais to her seat at the table. It wasn't a long walk but seemed twice as long to her as before.

The judge motioned for the two attorneys to follow him to chambers and Annette Bailey touched Maggie's arm and said quietly, "Don't worry, I think it will be okay."

Maggie tried to smile but just couldn't do it. She looked back toward the third row and saw Carolyn and Homer. He gave her a thumbs up. She wished she felt as confident as he and Annette Bailey did. Carolyn looked as anxious as Maggie felt, but managed a small smile for her sake. A smile she didn't feel any more than Maggie did when she returned it.

The judge and attorneys were in conference longer than she was comfortable with, having a pleasant break with coffee and croissants, but no one else knew that. She sat quietly and faced the bench after that brief look back at her friends who were the only family she had in this world. All the locals were wonderful to have said all those nice things about her, but it was Carolyn and Homer who'd stood by her through everything she'd ever gotten into since she'd known them. Of course, she'd known Homer almost half her life and Carolyn only a few years but she loved her housemate like a younger sister, someone she could tell anything to and not be judged harshly for it. And vice-versa. Of course, Homer had always been in her corner. Not to say they never had an argument in the past thirty some years. Of course they disagreed about things, but never anything so bad it drove a wedge between them.

When the door finally opened, she jerked her head toward it. She couldn't tell from their expressions what had transpired in there. All three of them looked serious. She wiped her damp hands on her slacks and tried to remain calm. This is it, Maggie. Now you'll know what the judge has decided. She braced herself for the worst case scenario, since he'd not asked her anything except why she did it.

Judge Fitzgerald sat at the bench and looked out at the courtroom for a moment and then he said, "Will the defendant please stand."

Bailey took Maggie's arm and guided her to her feet. She didn't say anything. At the other table, the prosecutor was looking straight ahead so Maggie couldn't tell anything from his expression, either.

"Maggie Metronia," the judge said, "after listening to all the testimony this morning and after questioning your motive for your dangerous actions on May 15, 2021, it is the judgment of this court to find you guilty of interfering with an official police murder investigation."

Maggie's knees let her down and she started to sink to the floor, but Annette Bailey and her second chair, Josh Mosley, helped her to remain standing. He handed her a glass of water and she drank a sip, but was afraid she'd vomit if she drank more, so pushed it back at him.

"And not to delay sentencing, because it would serve no purpose and I see no reason for a presentence investigation, either, I'm prepared to render my sentence at this time."

Maggie said nothing, but nodded her head slightly toward the judge. She felt as though she would cry if she had to utter one word, but she stood still and listened to him pronounce sentence upon her. She knew she was going to College Road. Not even the police lockup this time, as before.

"Maggie Metronia, with impunity, I sentence you to time served and two years of community service with the Key West Police Department to work in any capacity Chief Doan wishes to use you, for a period of no longer than eight hours a day and no less than four hours a day. You will report to Chief Doan on Monday morning and every morning at 8 this coming week. After that, Chief Doan will schedule your time, for however many days and hours he wishes, and in whatever capacity he wishes to use you for the next twenty-four months. Do you understand this sentence, Ms. Maggie?"

She didn't know whether to smile or look stoic, but she couldn't help it. The toothless smile burst through and she said, "Yes, your Honor, I do understand."

"Well then, I'll leave you to Chief Doan. Ladies and Gentlemen, this court is adjourned." His gavel came down and he left the room, his smile kept in check until he was alone in his chambers where she couldn't see him. "Maggie, I sure hope you've learned your lesson and that this ruse was not for nothing," he said to the empty room.

As soon as the gavel came down everyone in the room started clapping and cheering.

"Oh dear God, Maggie, you're free," Carolyn said, as she rushed over and hugged her close, tears in her eyes, because she also was afraid the judge would send her to the jail on College Road. Homer had still not confided to her that he had not paid the large bond when he left the courtroom with the officer who led him to the front door instead and told him to look serious when Maggie came out with Carolyn. He was never to tell her or anyone else it was not for real. She'd never asked to check the bank balance so she had no idea how much money she had in it, so the secret was safe with him.

"Yep, Mag, you're not going back to the hoosegow," Homer echoed in his own way, as he pulled her into his arms.

"You stay out of trouble now, Ms. Maggie," the Bahamian defense attorney Annette Bailey told her and even Sam Thomblin came over and shook her hand as he echoed Bailey's sentiments.

"Oh don't either of you worry. I've learned my lesson this time and I'll never interfere with an investigation, again, for as long as I live," she told them, with a big smile. Thomblin couldn't help but glance down to see if she had her fingers crossed behind her back, but her hands were both on the table. He smiled at her, and then walked back to the prosecution table, picked up his briefcase and walked out the courtroom door, with the smile still on his face. He couldn't wait to tell his beautiful Lola about his day in court. He didn't have to wait, as his wife had finished with her trial, also, and was waiting in the hallway for him.

"I caught some of it, and can't wait to hear it all," she said, laughing, as they kissed. "She looked like she was going to faint up there on the witness stand."

"I think Fitzgerald thought so, too," he told her, "which is why he asked Cookie to bring her a glass of water so quickly. What a fun day in court. I wish they were all this easy - and this phony." He smiled at her as they walked out to the car she'd parked at the foot of the steps again.

Nearly everyone in the courtroom came up to her and either hugged her or shook her hand. One of the ladies, Sheri Lohr, with her beloved service dog Champ on his leash beside her, said, "I'm so happy he gave you time served and community service, Ms. Maggie. Now you can work with the police legitimately without getting into trouble, again," she said, with a laugh, as she gave her a one armed hug, tugging Champ along with the other arm. "Let's go, Champ."

"Thank you, Sheri. I appreciate that and I hadn't thought about it like that, but I think I'll enjoy working with them instead of sneaking around on my own, hoping they don't catch me," she said, laughing with the younger woman, the publisher of SeaStory Press, who'd been on the island since the 1980s and wouldn't live anywhere else.

"I heard that, Maggie." She turned around and there stood Chief Lenny Doan, not smiling. "I'm going to work you hard so be prepared not to be pampered."

"I'm not afraid of hard work, Chief. Thank you for giving me this chance. I won't let you down."

"I didn't give you the chance, Judge Fitzgerald did, but I'm counting on it. I'll see you at 8 on Monday morning. And it wouldn't hurt if you brought a dozen or two of your chocolate chip cookies when you come in," he added.

"You've got it! I'll start baking early Sunday evening. See you Monday."

He turned to leave the courtroom, a smile on his face as soon as he was out of her sight. She had no idea how much of a ruse this whole thing had been from beginning to end, and for her own protection, she would never know. He, like the judge and attorneys, just hoped it has taught her to leave the detecting to the detectives from now on, before she does get herself killed being another Ms. Marple. "Oh, and a couple of your key lime pies wouldn't hurt, either," he called back to her, as he reached the courtroom door, his smile still wide as he left the courthouse.

I hope you enjoyed this third book in the *Bone Island Maggie Key West Mystery Series*. Maggie is a delight to write and can she ever get into trouble without the slightest provocation, even sneaking up on this author at times when I had no idea that was the direction her mind was headed. Honestly, I just go along for the bumpy ride and enjoy the gasps as she plunges headfirst into trouble and the laughs as she tries to talk her way out of deeper trouble – with the law.

Will there be a fourth book in the series? Are Maggie's sleuthing days behind her? Your guess is as good as mine. It probably depends upon how much she enjoys walking the line during her two years of community service with the KWPD.   *—PG*

ACKNOWLEDGMENTS

It is a rare writer who believes his or her work is perfect, after the first draft, without others checking it over before it is published. Kudos to such writers, if they believe this and their work proves them right, but for the rest of us, first readers are vital to our work. My thanks as always to my own first readers, my greatest friend Laura Smith and my wonderful sister Lela Buscemi. Many are asked, but few who are chosen enjoy or stick with the tedious task of reading manuscripts carefully to catch any errors, sentences or paragraphs that don't work. Laura and Lela have always been there for me as first readers and have been free with their comments so that before they are published, my books are as readable as they can possibly be, and I appreciate them so much for this. Another to join their little group was my youngest amazing daughter Suzy Herne, and that has made me the happiest! The last to become one of my first readers is another friend and good neighbor, Ray Ploen, whom I'm sure will become a valued first reader, also.

Thank you to my commissioner and friend when I was a Key West local, District Six Commissioner Clayton Lopez, for letting me use his name and having a little fun by promoting him to Mayor Lopez in my story.

Thank you, also, to reporter Mandy Miles and photographer Rob O'Neal, who also call Key West home, and who put up with this novice reporter when I covered the city commission meetings for a small newspaper and different websites when I was a local, and who agreed to be in my story on the scene at the dock to cover the shootout on the boat of the phony Dr. Tobin.

Last, but certainly, never least, thank you to my good friend Sheri Lohr, Publisher SeaStory Press, and her faithful companion, Champ, for appearing at the end of the book in the courthouse scene. If you look closely, in more of my books, you just might find Sheri and her fur companion or his predecessor, Pascal, somewhere within their pages, also.

Oh, okay, so there has never been a Hurricane Peggy or even a Tropical Storm Peggy in the history of named storms, and there never will be since the same names are recycled over and over. In this story, I took the tongue-in-cheek liberty of correcting that. Of course, there is nothing comical about the intensity of tropical storms and hurricanes, as too many of them are deadly monsters, and I don't treat them lightly in reality or in my writing. PG

ABOUT THE AUTHOR

As a resident of Key West for several years after retiring from a lengthy and diverse nursing career in 2002, Peg Gregory began a serious writing career, while covering the Key West City Commission meetings. For a period of time in the mid-1970s she left nursing and worked under the state attorney's office in Palm Beach County as acting coordinator of the newly formed sexual assault assistance program and paralegal counselor to survivors. She draws from both professions for most of her novels and award-winning short stories. She has written her memoir under Peggy Butler.

Gregory lives in Palm Beach County, Florida and has two daughters, four granddaughters, three great-granddaughters and four great-grandsons, whom, she admits, are the joys of this sunset of her life.

Reviews are the lifeblood of authors and they are how other readers learn of them, so please review this book at www.amazon.com or at the website of the bookseller from which you purchased the paperback or eBook. If you must write a negative review, the author asks just one thing of you, please be kind. Thank you!

NewAtlantianLibrary.com or
AbsolutelyAmazingEbooks.com
or AA-eBooks.com

Thank you for reading. Please review this book. Reviews help others find Absolutely Amazing eBooks and inspire us to keep providing these marvelous tales.

If you would like to be put on our email list to receive updates on new releases, contests, and promotions, please go to AbsolutelyAmazingEbooks.com and sign up.

For sales, editorial information, subsidiary rights information
or a catalog, please write or phone or e-mail

The New Atlantian Library
Manhanset House
Shelter Island Hts., New York 11965, US
Tel: 212-427-7139
www.AbsolutelyAmazingEbooks.com
bricktower@aol.com
www.IngramContent.com